LA Cinderella

AMANDA BERRY

First published in Great Britain 2011
by Mills & Boon, an imprint of Harlequin (UK) Limited,
Large Print edition 2011
Eton House, 18-24 Paradise Road,
Richmond, Surrey TW9 1SR

© Amanda Berry 2010

ISBN: 978 0 263 21803 9

Printed and bound in Great Britain
by CPI Antony Rowe, Chippenham, Wiltshire

After an exciting life as a CPA, **Amanda Berry** returned to writing when her husband swept the family off to England to live for a year. Now she's hooked, and since returning to the States spends her writing days concocting spicy contemporary romances while her cats try in vain to pry her hands off the keyboard. Her Marlene Award–winning contemporary romance, *LA Cinderella*, is her debut. In all her writing, one thing remains the same—love and happily ever after. Amanda lives in the Midwest with her husband and two children. For more about Amanda and her books, please visit www.amanda-berry.com

To my family and friends,
who help inspire me to be a
better writer, and especially my mom,
who gave me my first romance novel.

Chapter One

Natalie Collins tucked a strand of brown hair behind her ear as she shuffled down the hall. How on earth did she manage to get a job at Pandora Productions? Tall, swanky women and beyond-gorgeous men strode down the hall as if on a catwalk. It was hard not to gawk. Her conservative black pantsuit paled in comparison to the rainbow of colors.

The corner of a binder bit into her side. She shifted the two overstuffed binders, trying to balance them. Her glasses slipped down to the tip of her nose again. Of all the rotten luck, to have one of her contacts rip the day before the replacements arrived. Leaning her shoulders back, she tipped her head and tried to wiggle her glasses back in place. She shifted her load again to keep it from falling and ran into a wall.

Her glasses slid to the floor, but she kept hold of the binders. After steadying herself, she glared at the wall. Only the blob in front of her definitely wasn't a wall.

Oh, no, she'd run into someone, probably disrupting their strutting.

A hand gripped her elbow. "Are you all right?" The deep voice caused shivers to course down her back. "Let me take those."

The weight of the binders was lifted from her and she squinted to try to make the man in front of her come into focus. "I…I'm fine. I just lost my glasses."

"How very Velma of you," the voice said, followed by a chuckle.

The voice sounded so familiar, and Natalie's stomach started twisting. What if it was…no, it couldn't be. She heard the thud of her binders on a counter. The man-blob stooped down briefly.

Her heart sank as the glasses brought the face of her rescuer into sharp focus. Chase Booker. Unruly, sun-kissed blond hair fell on a face that angels would envy. Brilliant green eyes sparkled with amusement. A fan girl she was not. A squealing teenager she was not. A hot-blooded woman she unfortunately was.

So much for hoping he wouldn't be as attractive in person. She realized her mouth was agape and he'd put her glasses on her. A little piece inside of her trilled in happiness as his knuckles brushed her cheek.

Hot waves of embarrassment came up quickly, making her face burn. She closed her mouth. "Thank you, Mr. Booker. I'm terribly sorry I ran into you. I hope I didn't hurt you." Oh, somebody stop her from talking. Maybe the wall would open up and swallow her whole.

"No problem. Let me help you carry these."

"No, I've got it. Really." She tried to get there first and bumped up against his side. She knew from his last movie exactly how ripped that side was and the rebellious little piece inside her squealed in delight. She was really going to have to have a talk with herself when she got out of this.

"I insist."

With that face and that body, he could pretty much insist on anything and get it. Her face was probably as red as a beet by now. She dropped her gaze and backed away.

His smile took her breath away. "So where am I taking these?" He held the binders with one arm. His eyes met hers and she had to resist the urge to sigh.

She knew why so many leading ladies went out with him. One look from those emerald eyes and they were goners. She fussed with an imaginary piece of lint to break the contact. "To accounting. My desk is outside Mr. Morrison's."

"You're new to Pandora Productions." It was a statement of fact, so Natalie wasn't sure she was supposed to answer. He led the way down the corridor.

Natalie fought to keep her gaze on his broad shoulders and off his legendary butt. Also very prominent in his last film. She cleared her throat. "Accountant. I'm the new accountant."

He set the books on the desk and turned back to her. Could beauty blind? He held out his hand. "Welcome on board."

She took his hand and a pulse ran through her. Would she ever get her face to stop burning? Probably not with him around. "Thank you, Mr. Booker."

"Call me Chase." He released her hand.

Had he held her hand a little longer than normal?

She gripped her own hands together tightly. Attraction to a magnificent man was perfectly normal. She would definitely get over it after working with him for a while. After all, he was probably spoiled, used to getting what he wanted, overbearing and his eyes were gorgeous. She had to snap out of it. "Thank you… Chase."

He smiled again and she could have sworn she saw a spark of interest in his eyes. Not possible.

"I look forward to working with you…"

"Natalie Collins."

"Natalie." The word rolled off his tongue like a caress. Her knees turned to jelly. It was one thing to drool over him in a movie, but to drool on her boss wasn't professional at all and not a good way to start a business relationship.

She had better get over this quick.

With a cup of steaming black coffee in one hand, Chase Booker stared at the mounds of paper on his desk. Two months of filming on location had taken its toll on the wooden surface. He swallowed some of the hot liquid and glanced at the clock.

In five minutes Martin Morrison, his CFO, and Robert Addler, his partner, were supposed to come in for a meeting. The warmth of the coffee filled him even as the caffeine seeped into his veins. His flight from London had been delayed, so he was dealing with jet lag and fatigue.

The shoot had gone well and even though his production company, Pandora Productions, hadn't produced the action film, he'd loved every minute of it. Especially his married costar. For once he hadn't had to pry off the tentacles of an actress trying to make a name for herself.

After the breakup with Alexis Brandt, he needed something different. It was always the same. Some attractive, no-name actress needed a step up from the D list to the A list. Knowing his track record for giving his girlfriend that extra boost to her career, the actress sets her sights on him. Regardless if he was single or still involved.

He rubbed the bridge of his nose. Maybe it was time for something different. Large brown eyes behind glasses flashed in his mind. The little accountant. Barely over five feet tall. Her brown hair pulled back in a ponytail.

He smiled. In the movies, the librarian takes off her glasses and lets down her hair and she's the most beautiful woman alive. Natalie Collins may not be that type of beauty, but there was something about her. He couldn't put his finger on it.

Maybe the jet lag had gotten to him, but she seemed like the type of woman he wouldn't mind coming home to. Soft eyes not jaded by Hollywood. An innocence the women he went out with only pretended to have. Totally wrong for him, and he was totally wrong for her.

Even if the spark of awareness hadn't been

so intense, he still would have found himself captivated by the upturned corner of her pink lips. He'd been down that path before. A path he had no intention of going down again.

A sharp rap on the door brought him out of his brooding thoughts.

"Come in."

Robert came through the door first with his trademark easy smile and loose gait. Chase stood and gripped the hand he offered.

"Good to have you back." Robert's hand tightened on his.

"It's good to be back. I missed the sun."

Robert stepped back and Chase noticed Martin lingering in the doorway.

"Martin. How's our company doing?" Chase gestured for the man to come in.

"How was your flight, sir?" Martin came forward and sat in the chair, shuffling his papers. He never met Chase's eyes. Robert had assured Chase it was just him. When Chase was gone, the CFO didn't act like a mouse in front of a cat. Star envy or some such bull.

"A hassle, but it's over." Chase sank into his chair as Robert sat next to Martin.

"How was filming?" Robert sprawled back in the chair. "Another Oscar award-winning performance?"

"I don't think *Assassin's Target* is Oscar-caliber, but it was great to get back out there. I forgot how much I missed it. The money was nice, unlike *Night Blooming*." Their production couldn't seem to find its way out of the red into the black.

Martin cleared his throat and shuffled through his papers again.

"Do you have the numbers, Martin?" Chase glanced at the stack on the man's lap.

Martin riffled through and pulled out two sheets. His hand shook as he handed one to Robert and passed one across the desk. "These are the preliminary numbers. There are still a few receipts outstanding and a couple of expense reports we are waiting on."

Chase glanced down. The numbers above the line didn't tell him much, but the number in parenthesis at the bottom indicated they'd run over by a hundred thousand dollars instead of making money. He slammed the paper down on his desk, causing Martin to jump.

"How can this be?" He met both men's eyes before looking at the paper again. The numbers hadn't changed. "*Night Blooming* was number one at the box office for several weeks, plus the early release to DVD. The Golden Globe nominations and the Oscar talk. We should be in the black, not the red."

Martin shifted in his chair. "There were costs we hadn't anticipated."

"How could that be?" Chase leaned back in his chair. Every extra dollar counted. The loss would mean one less project they could back this year. "This isn't our first film. Robert, you came up with the budget. You're not green."

"I don't know, Chase," Robert said. "My budgets are pretty tight. The only thing I can think of is to have accounting look into it."

Chase turned back to Martin.

Martin cleared his throat. "Um. I hired a new assistant who will be auditing this budget first thing. I need to start working on the financial reporting for the month."

The little accountant. His pulse jumped. "This is our priority, Martin. We need to get to the bottom of this."

"Natalie!"

Natalie cringed as Martin barreled toward her desk. The CFO liked to yell at her when telling her to do something. He wasn't demeaning or anything, just loud. If anyone was nearby, they always turned to look.

"Yes, Mr. Morrison?" She placed the papers in her work tray and waited for the next project about to be yelled at her.

"Come into my office." He pounded past her desk and into his office.

She grabbed her notebook and pen and followed him.

"Close the door."

She shut the door and sat down across from him, her pen ready. The reams of papers and folders built up on Martin's desk looked as if at any moment they could topple over. He slammed the files down on top of one of his stacks. She jumped. A few papers lifted slightly but didn't dare move from their assigned spots.

He turned as if just noticing her. His brown eyes narrowed and then cleared. "Do you remember when I interviewed you how I told you we need to audit the expenses on productions?"

"Yes, sir." Experience she needed if she wanted to move up in the accounting field. She hadn't wanted to go into audit or tax after college like many of her classmates. She wanted to be like the man in front of her. Well, maybe not exactly like him, but the opportunity to be more than just a staff accountant had been irresistible.

Reaching behind him, he picked up a large folder and handed it across the desk to her. He leaned down, picked up a binder and another folder twice as thick and passed them, as well. The pile on her lap now reached her chin.

"Print out the expenses on *Night Blooming*. These should be all the files, but you may have to pull some more out of the drawers. Go through each expense and make sure you have a corresponding paid invoice and that invoice is for *Night Blooming*. It should have a charge number and be signed by myself or Robert Addler. Any questions?"

"No, Mr. Morrison."

"You've been authorized to work overtime to get this done. I expect you to work at least fifty hours this week and next."

"Of course." It was already Tuesday. She'd

only worked seven hours yesterday because Mr. Morrison had sent her home early. She'd have to work over ten hours a day for the remainder of the week to catch up. Not that she had much to go home to. Her roommate, Rachel, who had a life, was always traveling or staying out late.

"Put aside everything else. Mr. Booker wants the numbers as soon as possible."

The sound of his name sent a little shiver through her, but she shook it off.

Martin waved his hand in dismissal, and Natalie hefted the files into her arms. Balancing them precariously, she opened the door and managed to make it to her desk without losing anything. The stack looked imposing as she sat behind it.

Pulling out her keyboard, she typed in the parameters to run the report. She glanced up as Chase's door opened and he stepped out. Her stomach tightened. So much for an easy week.

Chapter Two

Natalie had to go home. The pile of expenses looked as large as when she started, but her stomach growled and her vision was getting blurry. Her computer clock read 8:00. She started to restack her work so she would know where she was in the morning.

Everyone else had already left, including Mr. Morrison. A door opened and footsteps sounded on the tile floor. Her pulse leapt. Who else was here this late?

Startled, she stood to glance down the

hallway and saw the broad shoulders of Chase. Her pulse jumped again as she sat back down. She hurried to get her purse from the bottom drawer. Maybe she could beat him out and not have to talk to him. She was so tired she was bound to make a fool of herself.

Sliding the drawer shut, she tried to move away, but her pant leg had caught in it. She cursed silently and bent down to fix it.

"I thought I was the last one here." Chase's voice rippled over her spine like a light caress.

Darn it. "I was just leaving." Her pant leg freed, she looked at Chase and her breath caught. Even fatigued, he was magnificent.

His smile lit his face. "I'll walk you out, then."

Wait…what? "Okay." She could do this. She'd walked to her car with coworkers before. Of course, none of them made her feel weak in the knees and tingly in places she'd rather not mention.

Her hand shaking, she reached to turn off her desk lamp, but it tilted to the side. His hand reached out and steadied it before it fell.

"I got it."

Was there a shade deeper than beet-red? She clung to her purse as if it were a shield as she hurried around the desk. She barely came up to his chin. Not that she wasn't used to being short; it was just that he made her aware of how small she was compared to him.

"So how long have you been working here?" he asked as they started to walk.

"About a month now."

Reaching around her, he flicked off the light for the hallway they'd just left. Her nose filled with his subtle cologne, spicy and rich, tantalizing. She wanted to lean into him and… Whoa.

"Do you like working for us?" He didn't seem to notice her distraction.

"Yes, it's a great opportunity."

They stopped at the door to the outside.

Before he could reach across her again, she flicked off the switch and smiled uncertainly.

The only light came from the emergency backup in the corner. His hand gripped the doorknob, and he stopped. His eyes gazed down into hers, and the air was sucked out of the room.

His mouth opened as if to say something but then shut again. Her heart hammered against her chest. Finally he smiled and turned the knob.

"Sorry, I'm a bit jet-lagged." He held the door open while she passed through. He closed the door and locked it. "I had to get through some files on my desk. If I'd been at home, I'd already be in bed."

An image of him on black satin sheets raced through her mind. She swallowed hard. "Well, I won't keep you. My car's right there. Good night, Mr. Booker." She started to walk away.

"Chase. Good night, Natalie."

She could feel his eyes on her back as she walked. Almost dropping her keys, she finally got the car door unlocked and slipped inside. She glanced back to where he stood in the streetlight.

He appeared puzzled about something, but he smiled and his face cleared. He lifted his hand and waved. She waved back and pulled out of the parking lot.

Ignoring the man in a parked car with a camera strap around his neck, Chase punched in the gate code and pulled through. The garage door opened and he pulled the BMW into its spot next to his Aston Martin. He wasn't surprised to see the paparazzi on his street. They practically lived here with so many big names on the block.

He'd only let the paparazzi get to him once before he realized that his life really was different from everyone else's. Back when he was just a boy in love with a girl.

He walked into the dark kitchen. Its massive size and the lack of light made it cold and unwelcoming. Maybe sleep would help get his little accountant out of his head. Natalie's large brown eyes sat in his mind like a warm beacon. Most likely due to jet lag.

Distraction was needed. In the morning he'd wake up and figure out where to go this weekend, who to go with and who to leak the information to. With a new movie in the editing room, he needed his name to be on the tip of everyone's tongue.

Going out with him was a first-class ticket to any actress, but hell for a normal girl like Natalie. His high school girlfriend, Becca, had been like Natalie. Not looking for glory or her fifteen minutes in the limelight. Becca couldn't handle the spotlight. The people digging into her past and her family's past to figure out why Chase Booker, son of three-time Academy Award-winning Matt Booker and screen diva Madeline Caine, was interested in her.

In the spotlight before birth, Chase grew up and became used to the attention. Unfortunately Becca hadn't.

He checked the answering machine.

"Hi, Chase. Alexis. I heard you were done filming in London. We should get together this weekend. I'm also available Sunday if you still need a date."

Sunday was the Golden Globes. Alexis, like so many others, struggled to get ahead in a business where publicity was key. He'd liked Alexis and they had a great time together. He'd been a stopping point on her climb to fame, and when she decided it was time to move on, he hadn't wanted to stop her.

She knew how the business worked and hadn't minded the persistence of the cameras. In fact, she'd relished the attention. It had helped her land a starring role, but she wasn't the kind of woman he wanted to come home to.

When they broke up, he found himself wanting more. He wanted a woman who could be with him for who he was and not for the fame he could bring her. He wanted something simple for once in his life. He wanted someone who made him feel alive. And let him be just Chase Booker.

His attraction to Natalie was something new and unexpected. She tantalized his senses and pretended not to be interested. It intrigued him and made him want to explore further, but he had no right to bring her into his life and into the sharp focus of the camera lens.

By Friday, Natalie was ready to pull her hair out. The numbers swirled in front of her eyes even while she slept. Her contacts hadn't arrived, and she was tempted to duct-tape her glasses onto her head to keep them from falling down.

The government could come in and declare her desk a disaster zone. Precarious stacks of papers covered every available surface and spread out along the floor. She'd been over the numbers a hundred times, but still couldn't get to that final number. Something was missing.

"How's it coming along?" Martin shut his door and turned the key in the lock. Even though she was staying late, he left every day at five o'clock on the dot.

"I've got a few more accounts to go over and the expenses that just came in. I also have the actors' expense reports." She moved a paper from one pile to the next.

"Very good. Here's a list of all the actors who worked on *Night Blooming.*" The list was three pages, each filled with double columns of names. "Some of our extras had expenses, too."

Natalie stifled a groan as she thought of all the expense reports for the six months of shooting.

"Have a good weekend." Martin shouted behind him as he hurried toward the exit.

"Yeah, right," she said to herself. She set the

list aside and plunged back into the pile she'd been working on.

The next time she surfaced, she glanced at the clock. Almost eight. Every night, Chase had insisted on walking her to her car. She'd tried to work later and hoped he'd leave, but he'd wait. She couldn't leave any earlier or she wouldn't get her hours in, and she refused to work on Saturday.

Every night she figured was another opportunity to humiliate herself. It was only a matter of time before he caught her with a goofy grin on her face when she looked at him.

She'd seen him already today. Every time he'd walked past her desk, she'd stopped working and watched. She'd tried not to, but her nose would catch the faint whisper of his cologne, and her head would jerk up in response. And there it would be, his behind clad in denim. He wore jeans the way jeans were meant to be worn.

How many times did the man really need

to go past her desk during the day? Seriously. Sure her desk was in the main thoroughfare of the office, but still…

Every night it was awkward walking with him. He always asked how her day went and was amazingly nice. He seemed genuinely interested in her work life. She had hoped to be over her little infatuation, but the guy wasn't demanding and didn't expect star treatment.

He seemed really down to earth for someone who had a star on the Hollywood Walk of Fame and probably an Oscar or Golden Globe for every room of his house. Genuine. She hadn't expected him to walk her to her car or hold the door open for her.

She glanced at the clock again. She could sneak out a few minutes early, and she wouldn't have to see him again until Monday.

She slid her chair out and reached for her purse. The computer beeped as the screen went black. She winced and glanced down the hall toward his office. Nothing.

After grabbing her purse, she shut off the light and rushed down the hallway. Every few seconds she glanced over her shoulder to make sure he wasn't there. At the door, she heaved a sigh of relief.

With one last look back before opening the door, she was home free.

"Excuse me," a soft, feminine voice said.

Startled, Natalie let out a small scream and almost dropped her keys. Alexis Brandt stood in the now open doorway. From her blond hair to her perfectly manicured fingers, she was everything rich and fabulous. She was also Chase's last girlfriend. Ex-girlfriend, if the tabloids were to be believed. Natalie's roommate Rachel kept her informed of everything going on with her boss and everyone else in Hollywood.

"Is Chase still here?" Her voice was low and husky. Her perfume wafted in waves of floral scent to Natalie.

"I don't—"

"I'm here, Alexis." His voice was directly behind Natalie.

Her heart slammed against her chest. She'd almost made it. Alexis swept through the door, brushed past Natalie and wrapped her arms around Chase.

"Darling." She kissed the air next to his cheeks. "I was so glad you called."

Natalie tried to fade into the wall and slowly slide toward the open door.

"Natalie." His voice was stern as if she'd done something wrong. Sure she'd tried to sneak out before he had a chance to walk her out, but he obviously had his hands full now.

"Yes?" Natalie didn't dare turn around and watch the blonde pressing her over-endowed body into his.

"Wait here for a minute." His words were directed at Natalie and he meant business.

She sighed and gazed longingly at her car a mere half block away in the parking lot.

"Natalie?"

She glanced back. Alexis had moved behind Chase, feigning interest in a picture on the wall. Chase's eyes warned Natalie not to disobey him.

"Yeah, I'll wait." She let the door slide closed and leaned against the wall as Chase led Alexis down the hall to his office.

He was her boss. She shouldn't be acting this way, but every time he came near her, her instincts said *run*. Every time he accidentally brushed against her or held the door open, she couldn't help thinking he was interested in her, which couldn't happen in a million years. But it confused her and she didn't like anything confusing in her life. She stared at the second hand on her watch.

He'd only said to wait a minute. She glanced to make sure he wasn't coming yet. When a minute was up, she was out of here. Thirty seconds. She'd have all weekend to try to get over her crush on him. Twenty seconds. Almost there, come on. Fifteen. Ten.

Chapter Three

Chase smiled as Natalie leaned against the wall staring at her watch. Probably counting down the seconds. His little accountant had tried to leave without him. He justified walking her out every night because she left so late.

But in reality, he just wanted to be close to her. Even if he couldn't think about being anything more than her boss, he couldn't resist the calmness and sweetness she exuded in spite of her nervousness. Not to mention the gentle swaying of her hips, the curve of her calves.

And he could feel like just a normal guy walking a girl to her car.

She was so focused on the watch she didn't hear him slip up next to her.

"Ha." She smiled and looked up. The smile disappeared and a look of chagrin crossed her face. "Oh."

"You do know this neighborhood isn't safe at night."

She dropped her eyes and her fingers fiddled with her purse. "I guess."

He leaned across her to push open the door. Awareness singed him where her body brushed against his. The clean scent of her floated in the air with just a touch of sweet, fruity scent, maybe strawberry, from her hair. Her gaze jerked to his. Had she felt the sizzle, too?

Her tongue darted out to wet her lips. His body tightened. He fought against the urge to drag her into his arms and find out if her lips tasted as sweet as she smelled. She was his employee, and he was her boss.

Clearing his throat, he said, "How was your day?"

She took his offer of escape and slipped out the door. "It was fine."

Every night, it was "fine." He wondered if she would ever just tell him about her day. He'd seen her working hard all day long. Strands of hair had escaped her usual ponytail and fell softly around her face. His fingers itched to push it behind her ears or release it all from the ponytail and sink into the rich strands.

He followed her out to her car. Her blue business suit and low heels were a refreshing change from the plunging necklines and stilettos Alexis wore. During the day every time he saw her, his imagination ran rampant wondering what Natalie wore under those clothes. The cut of her suit left a lot to the imagination, and he had a great one.

"Thank you," she said, not turning. Her keys jingled.

"Natalie." He wanted to see her wide brown

eyes one more time to get him through his weekend spent with the privileged and the jaded.

The keys fell to the ground as she looked at him over her shoulder. Her eyes widened. He stooped down to pick up the keys, using the distraction to keep himself from kissing her until her eyes melted like chocolate.

He stood and handed her the keys.

"Thanks." Her cheeks and neck were red. How far did the blush go?

He stuffed his hands in his pockets. "Have a good weekend."

"You, too." She stared up at him.

Her lips were barely parted. Mentally, he shook himself. She worked for him and he was mooning over her like a teenager. *Move, you fool.* He backed up a step, giving her room to open her door and slide into her car. He walked back to the building, pausing to watch as she sped off into the night.

When he entered his office, Alexis pounced

from the chair. "There's this new part that I'd be perfect for. The Golden Globes are Sunday. If we're seen together there, it could help my chances. We can say we're still friends. We are still friends, aren't we?" She pouted her famous pout.

He sighed, thinking of the woman he'd just left who didn't want anything from him. Not even for him to walk her out to her car.

Alexis continued to chatter about going and being seen, but he couldn't concentrate on her prattle. What would Natalie do if he asked her out? What if like other stars he had a relationship that wasn't broadcast over every available airwave?

Alexis would serve his purpose of getting the paparazzi to stop guessing who he was going after next. He could see if this spark between him and Natalie could be coaxed into a flame, which was a ridiculous thought. Maybe he just needed a break from dating. Alexis would keep the other women at bay without putting the pressure of a relationship on him.

"Are you even listening to me, Chase?"

He brought his attention back to the woman seated across from him. Every hot-blooded male wanted Alexis and would do anything to go out with her, but Chase wanted more than stunning good looks. Innocence and intelligence wrapped up in a small frame lingered in his mind.

"Sure, Alexis. We can go and be seen."

"I have the perfect thing for this weekend."

Natalie rolled her eyes to the ceiling. "I'm not going out. I just finished working an eleven-hour day."

Rachel tended to be the life of the party and tried to drag Natalie with her. A habit that started when they'd roomed together in college and continued when they'd both decided to stay in L.A. after graduation. Rachel would just have to go without her this time.

Rachel came out of the kitchen holding a stack of DVDs and a bowl of popcorn. "Nope, we're staying in. I've got ice cream in the freezer, too."

"Chocolate?"

"Of course. Pick the first movie." Rachel tossed the DVDs on the couch next to Natalie.

Picking up the first one, she groaned. *She didn't.* Natalie spread out the three DVDs. Emerald eyes stared at her from the cover of every DVD. *She did.* Natalie sighed in resignation—so much for getting Chase Booker out of her mind this weekend. She picked up *Into the Hereafter.*

Rachel plopped down next to her. Her blue eyes sparkled with mischief. "I couldn't let you be the only one staring at that hot bod all day." She reached across Natalie and snatched *Riddle Beach.* She turned over the DVD. "This one has nudity. I vote for this one first."

"Fine." Just what she needed—an image of

what he looked like undressed for Monday morning. That wouldn't be at all awkward. *What'd you do over the weekend, Natalie? Oh, stared at your naked body on DVD.*

She grabbed the burgundy throw from the arm of the couch and helped herself to a handful of popcorn. At least there wasn't a chance of this Chase catching her looking at his hot bod.

The opening scene came on the TV. Alexis was the female lead in this movie. Her body flowed across the room with grace and elegance in her forties dress. Her outrageous red lips jumped from the screen.

Natalie's hand formed a fist around her blanket. "Alexis Brandt came by the office tonight." The words spewed from her mouth before she could stop herself.

"Oh, do tell. Dirt before it even hits the stands. How cool is that? Were they, you know, together?" Rachel tucked her legs under her.

She couldn't spend an hour without checking the entertainment blogs or news.

Tightness spread through Natalie's chest. Maybe she was coming down with something. She reached over for her drink and took a sip before answering. "I don't know. She did the air kiss, and I left them alone in the office."

"A little office nookie." Rachel's voice quivered with excitement. "Oh, I bet they are having sorry-things-didn't-work-out sex all over the office. I wonder if they'll go to the Globes together."

Natalie gagged on a piece of popcorn. Rachel thumped her hard on the back. Chase having sex in the office—yet another image Natalie didn't want in her brain for Monday morning. Or any morning, for that matter.

On the TV, Chase walked on the screen. Dressed in a long trench coat and derby hat, he sat at a table to watch Alexis's character sing a soulful version of "Fever."

"That's probably not even her voice," Natalie murmured under her breath.

"Is he really that good-looking in person?" Rachel didn't wait for her answer.

Of course, Natalie would have had to admit he looked better in real life. On screen he was larger than life, but in reality, he seemed like a normal guy. A gorgeous normal guy. She could feel the heat flood her cheeks from just thinking about him.

"We have to have lunch this week. I can come to the office to pick you up and try to snag a view of Mr. Sexiest Man Alive for myself."

"I don't think that's such a good idea. I have a lot of work to do next week." Natalie reached for another handful of popcorn.

Rachel was more Chase's type than she was. Her dark hair never had a strand out of place. Rachel also had killer curves. Natalie knew from experience that men wanted Rachel.

Not that Natalie wanted Chase to want her.

"It's just lunch. Nobody would fault you for

going to lunch. Besides—" she shoved her hand out toward the TV, "—you can't deny me my one opportunity to meet the man of my dreams."

Natalie snorted. "I thought the man of your dreams was Matt Damon."

"Well, normally, but since Matt isn't available I'll settle for Chase. C'mon, Natalie, you know you can't say no."

A fact her roommate used against her constantly. But one she wasn't willing to fight about right now, or anytime, for that matter. Confrontation made her ill. The camera pulled in tight to Chase's eyes, and she coughed to cover the sigh that tried to escape.

"You know I'll just keep pestering…"

"Fine, we'll do lunch, but I meet you at the door and if he isn't around, we leave. Now, can we just watch the movie?"

Rachel squealed and shook Natalie's arm, knocking popcorn all over the floor. "I get to meet Chase Booker. Oh, this is the scene where he walks across the room naked. Shhh."

Natalie wanted to roll her eyes, but couldn't take them off Chase's body. It had to be touched up in editing or a body double. No one could look that good in real life.

Of course, Monday morning, Natalie found herself staring at Chase as he walked by. The images from the movies played in her head. She tried to detect a difference in the walk to see if they'd used a body double. But his swagger was definitely unique and the perfect butt was again outlined in jeans that should be a sin for him to wear.

"How's the audit going?" Martin's stern voice rang out behind her.

She jumped in her chair. Her face flushed from being caught watching the owner's butt as he strolled down the hallway. Picking up a few papers, she turned. "I've been making progress. I've pulled all the expense reports and started itemizing them in a spreadsheet."

His mouth tightened. "Good. I expect you to continue working late until we get this thing figured out."

"Yes, Mr. Morrison." Though it wasn't really "we" working this out.

He nodded to her and returned to his office. Turning back to her desk, she lost herself in expense reports for all sorts of weird things: haircuts, manicures, massages, personal trainers. Not so weird for a Hollywood production, but really weird to her, especially the amounts for each one.

When she got to a claim for toilet paper, she stopped. Sliding off her glasses and setting them on the desk, she closed her eyes and rubbed them. The numbers had begun to swim on the page. In her business class, they'd gone over legitimate expenses. Even though this was a movie set, the expenses were ludicrous. Who needed twenty-four dollars' worth of toilet paper for two days at a shoot? Maybe he had diarrhea. She smiled slightly.

"You look like you're in a good mood." Chase's voice curled around her ear and slid down her back, leaving a pleasant shiver in its path.

Resisting the urge to groan, she uncovered her eyes to stare at the blurry blob of Chase Booker.

"Did Velma lose her glasses again?"

She could hear the smile in his voice. Patting the desk in front of her, she gripped her glasses and forced them back onto her face. Maybe she'd have been better off not wearing them. At least when he was a blob, the only thing seducing her was his voice.

"No, I was just…" Her gaze dropped down to the huge amount of paper on her desk.

"Trying to find your way out of the recycling bin?"

Her gaze met his. The smile on her face froze as the unbidden image of him naked on the TV screen flashed in front of her eyes. The heat crept up from her chest until she swore it was going to pop out of the top of her head.

"I like it when you do that." His voice was soft and intimate.

Oh, God. What did he like? That she was visualizing him naked? Was she that obvious?

"There it goes." His eyes sparkled.

"What?" she managed to get her thick tongue to say.

"Your smile."

Seriously, flames should be bursting from her skull any moment. Her papers—she could look at her papers. Numbers didn't make her heart race, her palms sweaty or her mouth dry. She couldn't take her eyes from his, though.

"Have lunch with me."

"What? Why?"

When he smiled, his eyes lit from within and crinkles formed at their corners. Why was he asking her? Did he do that with all the employees? Was she reading too much into his question? Was his interest in her only as an employee?

"There you are, Natalie. I waited up at the front like you said, but… Oh, hi." Rachel stopped next to Natalie's desk, turned on her hundred-watt smile and tossed her perfect black locks over her shoulder.

Natalie kept her eyes on Chase, trying to read his expression. Once men saw Rachel, Natalie became invisible. Or worse, they pretended to be interested in her to get close to Rachel.

She knew she shouldn't have let Rachel talk her into lunch.

"I'm Rachel McAllister." She stuck out her hand to Chase.

"Chase Booker."

Rachel didn't let go of his hand right away. Natalie's stomach clenched. Even though she knew Chase couldn't be interested in her as more than an employee, she didn't want him to be interested in Rachel.

"You were in our apartment all weekend." Rachel smiled as she released his hand.

Natalie choked back a groan and wished the paper would come alive and eat her whole right this minute.

"'Our apartment'?" Chase raised an eyebrow.

"Natalie and I had a movie fest this weekend." Rachel kept grinning. "We watched all your movies. Since it was newly released we watched *Night Blooming*, even though you weren't in it. The award ceremony was spectacular. I loved your tux. Congrats on the wins." She batted her eyelashes up at him.

Natalie pushed back her chair abruptly and stood. Her boss did not need to know that she'd ogled him all weekend. "We were just heading to lunch. We'd better hurry if you want to get back to work on time."

Rachel turned bright blue eyes to her. "We don't have to leave right now."

Ugh. Natalie didn't like the look on Rachel's

face as Rachel turned her smile back to Chase. Frustrated, Natalie blew her bangs out of her face and glanced at Chase. His teasing grin had returned.

"Thank you," he said politely to Rachel before turning back to Natalie. "So, Natalie, which movie was your favorite?" His interest was far too intense. Was it because of Rachel or because he was interested in her?

Resisting the urge to shrink behind Rachel's tall figure, Natalie quickly ran through the titles in her head, trying to remember which one he was completely clothed throughout the entire film. "*Night Blooming.*" Ha.

His eyes focused in on her lips and she realized she was smiling. His comment earlier froze the smile on her face. What if he really liked her?

"Don't be silly, Natalie. Of course, she loves *Riddle Beach.* I mean who doesn't." Rachel's eyes practically devoured Chase. "After all, how often does a woman get a feast for her eyes?"

Screw the papers; maybe the floor would swallow her whole. She tugged on Rachel's arm, trying to get her to back off and just go, but Rachel jerked her arm back.

"I figured Natalie's favorite would be *If Only*."

Her eyes snapped up to Chase's face in amazement. To be honest, it *was* her favorite. She loved the story. The love, the purity, it gave her body tingles just thinking of the kiss at the end. Such perfect buildup, such beautiful emotions. Such an unattainable love.

Her mouth opened, a thousand questions on her tongue tumbling over each other to find their way to the surface. She clamped her mouth shut before they spilled out.

She managed to get out, "We should go."

"Natalie, stop being rude. Of course, Natalie loves that one, too. It never leaves the DVD player. That last scene… Natalie, what's that last line?"

Natalie pressed her lips together. Not that Rachel would notice, as her full attention remained on Chase.

Rachel continued without even blinking an eye. "Oh, what is it? There's that song going on in the background, and she's almost out the door, but she stops when he says it? Natalie, you know what it is."

"'I can't lose you.'"

Natalie's head jerked up at Chase's voice. He wasn't looking at Rachel. He was looking at her. His green eyes touched her so deep. Her breath caught in her throat.

"Yeah, that's it. But there's more," Rachel said.

Chase continued as if Rachel weren't there. "'I'd give up my entire world for one more moment in your arms. One more night by your side. I want it all. All of you. I want you to have it all. All my love, all my heart, all of me.'"

Her purse hit her foot, jerking her out of the moment. It felt like he was really saying it to her, not Elizabeth, the heroine in the movie. Which was ridiculous even to think. Actors acted. He was just acting. She pressed her glasses back up her nose and reached down to pick up her purse.

"Wow, you are good." Rachel's appreciation was too much for Natalie. This whole situation was too much for her.

"Let's go, Rachel. Chase has more important things to do." Again Natalie took hold of Rachel's arm. "'Bye, Chase."

"Okay, okay, I'm coming." Rachel finally took the hint. "It was nice meeting you, Chase."

"Natalie?"

She risked looking at him again. The flames

engulfing her face hadn't died down the entire time. "Yes?"

"Think about what I said." He nodded to Rachel and headed down the hallway.

Chapter Four

Think about what he said? How could she think of anything else? Even with Rachel prattling on across the table about how surprised she was that Chase looked that good in real life, she couldn't get those words out of her head.

Maybe he didn't mean to make her obsess about the ending lines that gave her that feel-good feeling when she needed a pick-me-up. Seriously, the man did not need writers making him sound romantic when he could just say "come here" to a woman and she'd be all over him. But if it wasn't that, what else had he said?

Besides, the kind of love found on the movie screen was nowhere near what real life was like. Men like Chase didn't go for women like her unless something more was going on, or it was part of a script.

"Oh, on the blogosphere this morning, Chase and Alexis were seen at Hyde on Friday night and at Spago on Saturday. Not to mention the Golden Globes. God, I wish I had her body and that dress. Wow." Rachel took a bite of salad. "Mmm. Their reps wouldn't comment on their relationship. You know what that means?"

Maybe it was lunch. That's right. He'd asked her to lunch sometime right before Rachel had appeared. Probably a thing he did with all new employees. It wasn't like she was special in some way.

"Natalie. Natalie!"

"What?" She focused on Rachel's eyes.

Rachel's eyebrows were raised and she stared at Natalie like she was from outer space.

"Where are you?"

"What do you mean? I'm right here. With you. Having lunch." Natalie glanced down at her plate, surprised to find it still full.

"No, you weren't. You were in la-la land." Rachel speared a cherry tomato with her fork. "Besides, you didn't answer my question."

Natalie sifted through the last bits of conversation she'd heard. Something about Alexis and Chase? *You know what that means?* "What does it mean?"

"It means that Alexis and Chase are on again. That's the way of the world, you know. They break up, and then after their next big movie, they get back together and finally get married. Maybe have a kid, if it's fashionable at the time. Then have a messy divorce where they swear they'll stay friends for the children."

"So, Alexis and Chase are an item again?" Natalie ignored the knot in her chest.

"Of course. But they won't say anything about it for a month or so."

"Oh." She tamped down the disappointment that rose to the surface. She knew she'd been dreaming, but... Okay, so she'd hoped a little of his attention had been because of that spark in his eyes. Not that she was any good at reading men, but maybe, just maybe someone like Chase for two seconds thought of someone like her.

She stabbed her fork into a pile of lettuce and shoved the whole thing in her mouth. It tasted bitter.

Uh-oh. Natalie reread the numbers and double-checked the signatures. *Uh-oh.* She picked up the expense report on top of the other stack and lined up the signatures again. Not good.

"I'm heading out."

She snapped the papers together and leaned over her stacks as Martin walked out of his office. Wide-eyed, she tried to keep her face neutral and forced a slight smile.

His eyes narrowed slightly. "Is there anything you need?"

"Of course not. Why would there be anything I need? I'm good. I'm real good." *Stop babbling!* Clamping her lips together, she smiled tightly again.

"Fine." He tucked a newspaper under his arm and narrowed his eyes on her again. "How's the audit going?"

Realizing she was hovering over her work like a protective mother, she stiffly leaned back in her chair. Every night he asked the same thing and she was beginning to understand why. "Fine, I'm almost done with this stack and then I've got those over there to go through, but everything looks fine. Just fine."

"Well, as long as you finish by Monday. Chase and Robert want a full report." He locked his office door. "Have a good night."

He disappeared down the hall. She breathed

a sigh of relief. Glancing left and right down the hallway to ensure no one was watching, she picked up the last document she'd been working on.

After working through tons of documents with Martin Morrison's signature and handwriting, she was confident she recognized his writing. Paul Alan, an extra, had similar handwriting and had been paid in cash per Mr. Morrison's instructions.

So had another extra, Jan Robbins. The handwriting is what caught her attention. Both Jan and Paul had eerily similar handwriting, and it bore a strong resemblance to Mr. Morrison's.

She needed to know how cash payments were handled. Glancing over her shoulder at the closed door, she knew she couldn't ask Mr. Morrison even if he were here. If he were guilty of fraud, he'd know she was onto him, and she'd get fired. If she told him what she suspected and she was wrong, she'd still end up fired. Being fired a month into her first job would look really bad on her résumé.

It was after five-thirty on Thursday, which meant the office was practically empty with the exception of her. And possibly Chase. The office staff left early on Thursdays for happy hour.

She hadn't been alone much with Chase this week. Even though she felt relieved, that little part of her couldn't help being disappointed. The past few nights, Robert Addler had walked out with her and Chase, which was perfect for her. Chase couldn't bring up lunch again if they weren't alone. Unless it was purely business. So if he hadn't brought it up, did that mean it was personal?

Robert wasn't here today. She stood and stretched her stiff muscles. Maybe she could just root through the files and figure it out. She stared at the large filing cabinets that stored this year's bills. Four long drawers filled with paperwork sorted by vendor.

Maybe if she knew the rules on picking up cash and how it was given to the extras… She heaved a sigh. Walking around her desk, she stared down the hallway to the only light left on in the office. Her heart thudded against her chest. He would know how the process worked. Besides, she'd have to tell someone sometime. Someone above Mr. Morrison.

Wondering if she was making a huge mistake, she headed to Chase's office. Even with the little trill of anticipation to see him again, she walked slowly down the hall. Not only was she going to accuse the CFO, who had been here a lot longer than herself, of embezzling, but she had to make sure she didn't make a fool out of herself over Chase and her little attraction.

Every time she was near him, her body responded as if she were a cat in heat, and her brain went on vacation. She hadn't figured out how to control it yet.

Natalie paused outside the slightly open door.

His low voice reached her ears, freezing her hand in mid-knock. "Alexis, I don't think so.... No... I know how important this is to you, but I just... Yes... Have you tried Robert?... No, I'm not saying... If you would just... Sure, we'll talk tomorrow."

The phone click, as it was returned to the cradle, barely penetrated the fog in her brain. What did it mean? Were they back together? She rolled back on her heels and tried to slip back before he noticed her.

One step. She stopped at a rustling in the office, followed by footsteps. She squeezed her eyes shut. Oh, yeah, like that really hid her. She opened her eyes. A blue shirt filled her view. Oops.

Tentatively she raised her eyes to his bemused expression. As always, heat flushed through her and her heart slammed against her chest.

"Eavesdropping?"

"No, of course not. I was coming to ask you a question. Just a question. I didn't mean to over-hear.… Not that I heard anything… I mean…" Oh, God, someone stop her.

His grin seemed to increase the further she dug herself into the ground. Seriously, someone needed to make an emergency escape hatch one could fall into after one embarrassed one-self sufficiently.

"It's okay, Natalie. Come on in." He stepped back into his office.

He gestured to the leather guest chair before sitting behind the desk. She slid into the chair, and her eyes darted around the room. She crossed her legs and clasped her hands in her lap.

She'd never been in here before. The tiled floor from the hallway flowed into the nice-size office, not huge but bigger than Mr. Morrison's. Beige paint and framed movie posters covered the walls.

Finally her eyes rested on the man behind the

desk. Somehow he seemed closer than when he'd walked her to her car. Maybe it was his uninterrupted attention on her. A low thrum of energy sizzled through her body, and she involuntarily shivered.

"What was your question?"

Question? Oh, yeah, question. She'd had one. Things seemed to flit out of her brain when he was around. What had she been doing?

"Yes, umm…"

His mouth turned into a soft smile. "Take your time."

"Well…" She chewed on her bottom lip. Mr. Morrison. "When extras are paid in cash where does the cash come from?"

The smile faded from Chase's face, and he came to attention behind his desk. "We don't typically pay extras in cash."

Her hands tightened. "These are for expenses. You know, expense reports turned in and instead of a check they request cash?"

"Where are these expense reports?" Suspicion lurked in Chase's eyes.

She recrossed her legs and swallowed. "On my desk. I just noticed it today. Isn't that the way it's typically done?"

Chase stood and ran a hand through his hair. "Get the reports and meet me in the conference room. We need to figure this out."

"We?" she squeaked out.

He walked around the desk and gripped her elbow, helping her out of the chair and steering her toward the door. "Yes, we. Now, go get the documents, and I'll order us some Chinese."

"But I should go home soon." The conference room wasn't very big, so he'd be close, which made that little piece in her trill again. But if she were alone with him, she was sure to make a fool of herself. His hand on her elbow burned through the silk of her blouse. Why had she taken off her jacket? She'd definitely make a fool out of herself if left alone with this man for any length of time. But she did want to get to the bottom of this.

"Hot date?" Chase's voice sounded slightly gruff.

A fresh wave of heat swallowed her face. "No, but—"

His green eyes settled on hers. "I won't take no for an answer."

Chapter Five

By the time they were settled into the conference room, only two chairs weren't covered in papers. However, the chairs were right next to each other. If Natalie moved that stack…

Before she could move anything, Chase spoke up.

"Sit down and we'll discuss what you've found while we eat." His tone was all business. Maybe she'd read too much into their earlier conversations.

She could be businesslike, too. Relieved, she

breathed deep and slid into the chair. When he sat down his denim-clad leg brushed against her cotton skirt. She sucked in a breath, but covered it by opening one of the takeout bags. She crossed her legs away from his.

"I wasn't sure what to get, so I got a couple of different things. We can share," he said.

She picked up the containers and opened them. The rich sauce filled the air with the aroma of ginger and garlic. Settling on beef with broccoli, she found one of the rice boxes.

"What have you found so far?" Chase said. His leg brushed against hers again. Her body tensed. She wondered if he did it on purpose. His warmth radiated to her side. The woodsy smell of his cologne wafted over her.

"The…uh." She cleared her throat. "Um, well, I was going through the expense reports and I noticed the handwriting was similar on a few of them and…" Should she tell him that she suspected Mr. Morrison wrote them? She closed her mouth. She didn't want to accuse an innocent man. She only knew that the numbers told her that someone might be taking money.

"And?" he prodded. His gaze bore into hers, but it suddenly softened.

What had they been talking about? Was there a woman alive who could resist him? He didn't even have to put forth any effort to be irresistible. That kiss—her eyes dropped to his lips. That kiss at the end of *If Only*. She could feel her lips separate. The red-hot wave flowed over her face. She dipped her head as her food suddenly was way too interesting. After all, there was white, brown and green.

Way better to look at that than the slight scruff along Chase's chin. She was definitely going to make a fool out of herself.

When she dropped her gaze to her food, Chase leaned back in his chair. Trying to draw out this timid woman was like digging for diamonds. It took forever, but he just knew something special was hiding in there.

He'd already begun to suspect his chief financial officer wasn't on the up-and-up. Every time Chase approached him, Martin shook and started prattling on about this and that.

Chase also suspected the reason Martin had hired Natalie was because of her timidity and lack of experience. What Martin hadn't figured on was the intelligence lingering in the depths of her gorgeous brown eyes.

Setting down the box of noodles, Chase studied the woman next to him. She drew him with her quiet strength and a warmth he'd never experienced before. She wasn't what Hollywood considered beautiful—few people were—but the delicate tilt of her chin, the gentle upsweep at the tip of her nose, her wide, innocent brown eyes and her lips, all drew his eyes and he found himself captivated by her.

He loved watching her lips curve into a smile, tighten when she was upset or part slightly on a breath. Real, that's what she was. He shifted in his chair. She jerked her head up again. Every nerve in his body longed for more contact than his knee against hers.

Women like her should stay as far away as possible from men like him. Even as he lost himself in her eyes, he could see her pushing him away. She might trust him in the beginning, but when some reporter speculated he was cheating, or when he was gone for months on a shoot, he'd lose her. Distance rarely made the heart grow fonder.

Her gaze fluttered down again, breaking the connection. He couldn't resist trying to have her. Just for a little while, not forever. Just enough to get her out of his system.

"Show me the expense reports you found." He cleared his throat.

Her shoulders relaxed beneath her cream blouse. He made her nervous, but he figured everyone did. She reminded him of a small bird ready to take flight at the least provocation, except when she was talking work.

She put aside the barely touched food and pulled forward some papers. She handed him the first two reports.

Her gaze never left his face while he looked over the reports. It was intense, but not sexual in nature. It was the stare of someone waiting for a connection to be made.

The handwriting was similar on both reports, just enough difference to prevent someone from questioning them if they went through on the same day. He noticed the signature authorizing cash payments. *Martin Morrison.*

"Let's separate all the ones authorized for cash payment first." When she started to pull more papers her way, he stopped her. "After we eat."

She nodded and went back to playing with the box of food. Her tongue swept over her lower lip. How soft would her lips be? He took a deep breath; it was going to be a long night.

After they ate, Natalie stood and cleared the table. Her slight body moved efficiently. She didn't overemphasize any moves, like some actresses. Her blouse was loose on her frame, but her skirt tightened at the waist, and the cut was tight to the legs. As she bent over the table, he couldn't help appreciating her backside.

It was going to be a *very* long night.

She straightened, and he noticed her everpresent blush. Would she ever not blush around him? Did he really want her to stop?

"I'll be right back," she said, as she walked out the door with the bags.

Chase took in the amount of paper. They had hours of work ahead of them. Natalie slipped back in and returned to her seat.

"If you want, you can go through that one while I go through this one," she said. Her eyes didn't meet his, and he could tell that she was struggling. She wasn't used to giving orders.

"Sounds good." Pulling the stack closer, he looked for the same signature on the front page. As the smell of brown sauce and egg rolls dissipated, the scent of strawberries and other sweet smells started to permeate his nose.

He glanced over at Natalie's bent head when he was about halfway through. Precariously balanced, her glasses had slid down to the tip of her nose. His fingers itched to push them back and brush the gentle curve of her cheek. Her finger pushed the lenses back into place.

He brought the paper in front of him back into focus. As the pile of cash payments grew, Chase's temper rose along with it.

Martin Morrison had come highly recommended. Chase couldn't imagine the slight man committing fraud against the company, but as the evidence kept mounting up, he couldn't deny it. The handwriting on all of them resembled Martin's. But without seeing them together, Chase would have never seen the similarities. Martin was in charge of accounting and therefore the checks.

He doubted Robert would have noticed the handwriting, but how had Robert missed so many expenses paid out to extras? He paused on the expense report for Dana Bradley. It was a cash payment of almost a thousand dollars, but all the expenses were below the fifty-dollar receipt limit they'd established to keep the files smaller.

Robert's signature was on it, just like the others. Too much like the others. Chase grabbed the last one and put the sheets together. They were exactly the same signature, no variations.

Not only was Martin stealing from the company, but he was forging Robert's signature, too. This explained why *Night Blooming* had lost so much money, and it made Chase skeptical of the other productions that hadn't been losses, but hadn't been as profitable as he'd expected.

Apparently, Martin had gotten greedy.

"Can I see one of your expense reports?" Maybe hers would have Robert's real signature and not forgeries.

Natalie pushed her glasses back up her nose as she handed him the one she was looking at. He compared Robert's signatures, and again they were exactly the same.

"Mr. Morrison gave me a list of extras when he gave me the files."

"Do you have that in here?"

She retrieved a larger document than he'd expected. When Robert and Chase had originally discussed the crowd scenes, they'd decided to use computer rendering for the people. But when other costs increased they decided it would be more economical and more realistic to use extras.

Extras who weren't supposed to turn in expense reports. "Are all these extra expense reports?"

Her gaze analyzed each pile for a moment. "All except those three."

"Okay, let's focus on the extras only. Keep a running total."

"Okay." She actually seemed excited by the idea of adding what had to be hundreds of numbers. Her eyes brightened, and she flipped on the adding machine.

Only a slight bit of pink tinged her usually red cheeks. That quiet feeling spread through his chest looking at her. The intelligence sparkling in her eyes drew him. If his life were a little simpler, he'd think nothing of coaxing this woman into his arms.

He shook his head and went back to work. The light tapping of keys followed by the ticking of the numbers printing lulled him as he kept adding to her pile.

"I think that's it." He leaned back. The piles had shifted from one side of the room to the other. Her rhythmic typing continued. Her finger trailed down the page. She typed in the number, then lifted the sheet and added it to the other pile.

"That's the last one." She pressed the equal sign and then pulled the tape out of the machine.

"What's the damage?" He leaned forward.

She studied the number and then handed him the paper.

"Five hundred thousand dollars? This can't be right."

She looked back at the piles. "I can add it up again to double-check." She pulled the stack she'd just added back over.

Without this amount, *Night Blooming* would have been around the initial projections. They would need to have everything together if they were going to accuse Martin.

His gaze went back to Natalie. Watching her work was better than hanging out at clubs by a long run, but when she started to trail her finger down the page, he covered her hand with his. Startled eyes met his. A faint tinge of blue had appeared under her eyes. Most of her brown hair floated around her face, framing it.

"You can rerun the numbers tomorrow," he said, gently. When her gaze flitted to his hand on hers, he reluctantly pulled it away. Standing, he reached his hand down to her.

She glanced up at him before sliding her hand into his. His body came alive, but he resisted every temptation to pull her into his arms. The gentle curve of her mouth was almost too much. As soon as she stood in front of him, he released her hand.

"Let's get these back to your desk." Grabbing a pile, he headed out the door, away from her sweet scent. He thought he caught the sound of a sigh as he left the room.

Chapter Six

Grabbing a stack, Natalie followed, too confused and tired to argue. Not that she would have. She passed Chase in the hall on the way to her desk. Her hand still tingled as if he still touched her. She rubbed it on her skirt when she was in the conference room.

She bent and picked up more reports. When she stood, her glasses slid down her nose. Tipping her head back, she tried to wiggle them back.

"Here, let me help."

Before she could protest, he gripped the sides of her glasses and adjusted them on the bridge of her nose. Her breath caught in her throat. She held the papers as a makeshift shield to keep her treacherous emotions at bay. He was just helping her. That was all.

As if he couldn't resist, his fingers trailed down the sides of her face. Her pulse jumped, and desire pooled in her core. Papers on the floor behind her blocked her automatic urge to retreat. Surely, he hadn't meant anything by it. Certainly he hadn't meant to make her feel desire.

He dropped his hands and took the load from her without a word. She released it, thinking he'd take it and she'd grab the next. Her breath passed out over her lips.

He set the papers on the table and turned back to her. Her mouth opened, but nothing came out. She'd seen the look on his face dozens of times. Her heart threatened to pound its way out of her chest.

That was the look he'd given the heroine right before he kissed her. A look that had invaded her dreams where she played the part of Elizabeth in *If Only*. This was where the music would crescendo.

But this wasn't a movie. Chase wasn't playing a character, and neither was she. He stepped closer until a mere breath separated them. Obviously giving her the chance to stop him.

She should stop him. She wasn't what he wanted. She couldn't be what he needed. She didn't want to be famous. But with that look in his eyes and those eyes on her, she didn't think she could bear to stop him.

The back of his hand caressed her cheek. Her head leaned into the warmth as his hand left a trail of fire in its wake. His gaze held hers captivated, as his hand slipped to the back of her neck.

One last chance to say something. Her pulse raced through her veins. She licked her lips.

One last chance to stop this. One chance, one taste, that's all she needed.

He closed the distance until a breath separated their mouths. Her hands came up and grabbed the front of his shirt. His mouth touched hers, a whisper of a kiss.

Her eyes fluttered shut, and she jerked on his shirt. His lips pressed against hers, gently touching, tasting. They were soft and full. Her heart was pounding so hard she was certain he could hear it.

Her mind swam in a sensual fog. Chase Booker was kissing her. Natalie Collins. His tongue met hers and her knees buckled. It wasn't just *the* Chase Booker kissing her, but this man. The one who opened doors for her, walked her to the car, made her feel pretty even with her glasses on.

But he shouldn't be kissing her. He was her boss. His mouth slid to her cheek and sent a searing bolt between her thighs. She pulled in air, desperately trying to surface. She needed space. She needed to think. Pulling back, she rested her forehead against his.

His jagged breathing matched hers. His thumb rubbed the side of her neck, sending an echoing ache through her. Lifting his head, he smoothed her hair back from her face.

She opened her eyes. His were filled with desire, need and frustration. Her body responded to his, wanting to invite him in.

"I should walk you to your car." His tone was cool. His hands dropped, and he turned.

Ice water splashed through her, cooling her overheated body. He hadn't meant to kiss her. Was he trying something for a new role? Had she just been convenient? Or something different?

Jerkily, she picked up a stack of papers and walked around him.

"I'll do that," he said.

She couldn't look at him or speak. She just continued down the hall to her desk. Her eyes burned with tears, but as long as she didn't talk or stop, she could hold them back.

As she set down the papers, she felt him behind her. His hands rested on her shoulders. She could feel the walls crumbling all around her. There wasn't a hole big enough to sink into.

"I'm sorry. I didn't mean to…" he started.

Her body started to shake.

"No, I did mean to, I just—"

"Stop, please. Just stop." The first teardrop crashed down on the desk. She felt so stupid for actually thinking a man like him would want her. She couldn't turn around. She couldn't see the look on his face. Jerking from his grasp, she went around the desk and grabbed her purse.

Without looking at him, she hurried down the hall. Tears blurred her vision but didn't fall. He was behind her, but he let her go.

She didn't stop until she was behind the wheel of her car. She'd been stupid to think someone like him would want someone like her. He'd stopped at the building door and stood there watching her.

She could still feel his lips against hers. Desire clung to her. She'd kissed Chase Booker. It was like going to the sun. She should have known that she'd get burned.

Chase purposely arrived late the following morning. He'd had a long talk with Robert about Martin after Natalie had fled last night. They decided to keep things normal for now, so Martin wouldn't suspect that they knew anything.

He hoped Natalie had time to get settled before having to see him. He'd acted impulsively last night and moved too fast, but he'd needed to know how she tasted.

It'd been more explosive than he'd imagined. He hadn't wanted it to end. It shouldn't have happened in the first place, but he definitely wanted it to happen again.

When he entered Pandora Productions, the

receptionist turned to smile at him like she always did, but froze and pretended to pick up a call instead.

Damn it. He'd hoped his foul mood wouldn't show, but he had no desire to act right now. No desire to force niceties. He only cared how one person was doing today.

When he walked past her desk, she wasn't there. He stopped in the hallway. Had she stayed home? Had he pushed her too far?

"Don't forget to get through the audit today. I have to leave early, but I expect it on my desk first thing Monday morning." Martin's voice carried into the hallway.

"Yes, Mr. Morrison," came Natalie's timid voice. "It shouldn't be a problem."

Chase continued down the hall before she came out. She was here. He'd almost expected her to take a sick day or something, but he was glad she hadn't. Maybe he hadn't screwed things up for the company and for himself.

They needed her to help with this audit. Who was he kidding, he needed her.

As he entered his office, he saw an envelope in the center of his desk.

Chapter Seven

"What the hell is this?"

Natalie had been prepared for Chase's reaction, but she'd thought he'd be relieved. She hadn't expected anger. She straightened the crumpled letter of resignation he'd tossed on her desk.

"I… It's obvious, isn't it?" She kept her eyes on the paper.

"No, it's not." He paused and his tone softened. "Damn it."

Her eyes jerked up to his. Anger and frustration poured off him. His usual smiling face seemed tired this morning.

"I don't have time for this right now. You will have lunch with me today to discuss this letter." He acted like *letter* was a four-letter word. Without waiting for her answer, he disappeared down the hall.

Natalie glanced down the other way to see if anyone had witnessed his blowup. No one was around. Relief flowed through her. Well, she knew it would be awkward to see Chase this morning. Whatever she'd expected, it hadn't been anger. He hadn't gotten that upset when she'd told him about the fraud.

She folded up the letter, which gave two weeks' notice, and stuffed it in her purse. She'd just have to give it back to him at lunch. It would be much easier to talk to him in a crowded restaurant than in his office alone or, worse, at her desk where everyone at work could see, and the memory of last night's kiss lingered in the air.

Tugging a pile of documents closer, she sighed and began adding up the numbers again. She tried to lose herself in her numbers, but her mind kept jumping from the fraud to the kiss. She hadn't known what to say to Mr. Morrison. *Yeah, Mr. Morrison, we found a bunch of expenses that just shouldn't be there. Don't worry, though. I'm fairly certain you were the one that put them through.*

Every squeak of Mr. Morrison's chair made her heart skip a beat. Already keyed up by the fact Chase had demanded she have lunch with him, she kept expecting Chase to pop in front of her any moment. Then, what if Mr. Morrison figured out what she'd discovered by sneaking up behind her and seeing what she was working on?

When her desk phone rang, a small scream escaped her throat. Maybe she should have just stayed home. Picking up the phone and glancing around to make sure no one had heard her scream, she said, "This is Natalie. How may I help you?"

"Hi, Natalie. This is Jared Anderson from *Element Magazine*. I hear you're new at Pandora and was wondering if we could meet for lunch sometime."

A reporter? Calling her? "Um, I don't think that's a good idea."

The man's voice remained cajoling. "Look, we could have a mutually beneficial relationship. But I don't want to discuss it over the phone. They can't be paying you that much."

"I'm sorry, but I don't think so." A flash of movement in front of her desk captured her attention. She looked up into Chase's eyes. Her lips parted. The spark of desire flared to life. Her whole being shook with the force of his gaze.

Jared's voice continued in her ear. "We're always looking for someone to help us find the good stories. We're not asking you to rat out your boss or anything. Just a bit of an inside scoop on how Chase runs things down there."

"I can't. Really. I don't know anything about…" Her gaze dropped from Chase's quizzical expression. What if he thought she'd called the magazine? "…that and don't really want to talk to anyone at your…" She glanced up at Chase. "…business."

"Why don't you write down my number? Just in case you change your mind—"

"I won't. Thank you for calling." She set the phone back on the cradle. The papers in front of her could be straighter and were a lot easier to look at than Chase at the moment.

"Let's go, Natalie."

Her heart leapt in her throat. She nodded slightly, still not making eye contact. Picking up her purse, she moved to follow him out of the office. She kept her head down, not wanting to meet anyone's gaze. Her pulse jumped as she brushed against him when he held open the door for her.

Her resolve to hand in her resignation increased. She couldn't be expected to work with this man and not want him. Maybe every other woman in the office wanted him and just coped daily with it, but she wasn't like those women. Maybe he'd kissed every one of them, too. Hell, he could have slept with all of them.

Her chest crushed in on her heart. Though she wasn't a part of the gossip mill at Pandora Productions, she was certain someone would have mentioned that particular trait of Chase's. Or Rachel would have told her, since that kind of behavior wouldn't have escaped the attention of people like Jared Anderson. Why would a reporter call her?

Chase's hand lightly brushed the small of her back, guiding her to his car. Her breath caught, and she stumbled a little. He gripped her elbow to steady her.

He stopped them. After a moment, she looked up at his chin.

"Are you okay?"

No. "I'm fine." She pressed her glasses back up her nose and examined the concrete beneath her feet.

When he didn't continue to the car after a few moments, she dared a peek up at him. The wind tousled his blond hair, giving him that just-rolled-out-of-bed look. Her hair whipped loose from its clip and slapped her across the face.

"Do you ever say how you really feel?" His hand smoothed her loose hair behind her ear. His touch sent tingles coursing through her body. He glanced over her shoulder and frowned.

She followed his gaze and saw Mr. Morrison standing next to the door, cigarette in hand. He lifted his hand and waved. Chase's lips tightened, but he didn't say anything, just steered her toward the car again.

Chase remained silent while they were shown to a private corner booth. They'd come in the back entrance and hadn't drawn any attention.

Sliding into the seat, Natalie knocked over an empty glass. Chase caught it before it rolled to the floor. Her skin flushed pink as he slid in after her.

The table was small, but she tucked herself as far away from him as possible. He didn't know whether to be frustrated or to laugh. What he really wanted to do was pull her back into his arms and keep her there for several hours. But he knew they'd both be better off if they repaired their working relationship and forgot about the tantalizing prospect of that kiss. At least until this mess with Martin was over.

She picked at the napkin and stared at the menu.

The sweet, clean smell of her lingered in his nose. His fingertips itched to turn her face up to his. He cleared his throat. Her gaze leapt up to his, her eyes wide and wary.

"Do you know what you want?" He smiled, trying to reassure her and calm her down.

Her eyes widened further, and she leaned away from him. She looked like she was ready to bolt.

"To eat, Natalie. What do you want to eat?" He picked up his menu. "I typically get shrimp scampi, but everything here is really good."

"I'm sure it is." Her eyes darted back to the menu. How could he make her relax?

The waiter stopped by and filled their glasses. They both ordered, and he left, leaving them quite alone in the secluded booth.

She started to fiddle with her fork. He laid his hand over hers, stilling her fidgeting. Her eyes were warm pools of chocolate as they met his, but her body tensed.

"I'm not going to pounce on you."

Panic and disappointment warred on her face before her shoulders dropped slightly. "I know," she said, as if she knew he'd never do something like that.

He wanted to shake her. His whole body ached to pull her into his arms again and prove to her that even though he said he wouldn't, he wanted to.

"Natalie." He waited for her eyes to meet his again. "You are a very attractive woman. No, don't deny it. I find you incredibly attractive, but—"

"There's always a but," she said under her breath.

He blew out a breath and took a drink of water. He'd never have this much difficulty on a set. Everything was scripted already. He knew exactly how the other person was going to react. Natalie eluded him. He couldn't figure out her character, couldn't put her into a category.

"As I was saying, you work for my company. I shouldn't have taken advantage of you last night." He should say he'd never do it again, but something stilled his tongue.

The moment their lips had met he'd felt something he'd never experienced before. Desire and passion had been full-force in the front, but something had lingered in the back of his mind keeping him awake all night pondering the feeling. He'd felt protective and possessive. Feelings he had no right to have, but she'd felt right in his arms. He couldn't say he wouldn't be tempted again.

"I could have stopped you." Her voice was barely above a whisper.

The hesitation in her voice increased his pulse rate. He had to change the topic. "Have you had a chance to go through the papers again?"

Her body relaxed, and her hands stilled. "Yes, and I came up with the same number. As soon as Mr. Morrison leaves for the evening, I plan to go through the bank statements and figure out if he used a check to get the cash or if he made a withdrawal."

The confidence she exuded when talking about her job always amazed him. The pink receded from her cheeks, and her eyes were animated. This is the way she should always be. This is the way she should be with him.

His body tightened, but he shoved the desire back. For now, she couldn't be a part of his life except through work.

He remembered the look on Martin's face in the parking lot. He wasn't sure if the man suspected anything was going on between them, but he wouldn't put it past Martin to say something to the press.

"We'll have to take things carefully, if the files continue to point to Martin." Chase turned his thoughts back to business, a much safer subject. "He has his fingers in everything at Pandora. Robert and I talked this morning. We'll need a list of every bank account he has access to."

"I was just hired to help out. He hasn't given me a lot of things to do or shown me much."

The waiter reappeared and set down their lunches.

"The biggest thing is what he will leak to the

press when he leaves. There's no telling what he'll make up or what he suspects." He hoped that was enough to warn her. He didn't want her to start with the two weeks' notice again. Martin probably wouldn't try to bring Natalie into it, anyway.

He needed to make sure Martin wouldn't insinuate anything. That look on the man's face when he'd seen them in the parking lot had worried Chase. Surely, Martin wouldn't think anything was happening between Natalie and Chase. Maybe he should stay away from her desk during the day.

They ate in silence. When the waiter removed the plates, Chase turned to Natalie.

"We'll need someone to help with the transition until we get a new CFO if Martin is implicated. Can I trust you to stay with us until then?"

She hesitated for a moment, and he held his breath waiting for her reply. "Of course."

"Natalie, will you give me—Pandora Productions—another chance? I think you have a brilliant mind and would be a great asset to our company."

The red crept up her cheeks. She nodded slightly and lifted her eyes to his. "I'll try."

Chapter Eight

Natalie sat on the edge of her seat, waiting for the clock to turn five. Mr. Morrison had left at the same time every day for the past month she'd worked here, but tonight he was supposed to leave early. With her luck, he'd probably stick around.

Chase had been avoiding her desk all afternoon. After the first hour of waiting for him to pass by her desk, she'd started to relax. She ignored the twinges of disappointment as time continued to pass.

It would be better for both of them if they kept their relationship purely work-related. She could forget how his lips had caressed hers and how the warmth had flooded through her from the touch of his hands.

The door slammed behind her, and she almost fell off her chair. Mr. Morrison locked the door and turned his shifty eyes to her. "I expect the report first thing Monday morning. Just because Mr. Booker took you for a long lunch doesn't mean you can neglect your work."

Her cheeks were on fire. "Of course not, Mr. Morrison. I've got the numbers tied into the expense reports and just need to categorize two more reports before I'm finished." She hoped he was convinced by her lie, because she could hear the tremor in her voice and could feel the tightness of her smile.

"Good. I'll see you Monday morning." He hefted his briefcase in his hand and was out the door before she could say anything else.

Now she just had to wait for the rest of the

office to clear out. Which shouldn't take long. Over half the staff hadn't come back after lunch and half of those remaining had taken off early. They had places to go and be seen.

Her phone rang. She stared at it for a moment. The caller ID came up as Unavailable. She really didn't want to talk to Jared Anderson again, but he wasn't the only one who had her phone number.

Tentatively, she picked the phone up from the cradle. "This is Natalie. How may I help you?"

"Nat," Rachel's voice yelled above the background noise. "Brian finally asked me out."

"Good for you."

Rachel had been trying to get Brian from work to ask her out for months now.

"Don't wait up, sweetie. I don't think I'll be home tonight."

"Be careful."

"Hey, sorry about the mess in the kitchen, I was experimenting last night with cupcakes.

Turns out I can't cook, so I picked some up at the store this morning. Would you mind cleaning it up? Just in case Brian and I end up back at our place?"

Natalie had seen the mess when she'd come home last night but had been too exhausted physically and emotionally to do anything about it. "Sure. Be safe."

"Thanks, sweetie. See ya." The line went dead.

She set down the phone and stood. Time to wander through and see who was left in the building. The hallway runway was quiet as she headed down to fill her water bottle.

She held her breath as she passed by Chase's closed door and breathed a sigh of relief when nothing happened.

After filling her bottle, feeling confident that no one was left in the building besides Chase and her, she stopped at his door and knocked tentatively.

"Yeah?" She heard from within. She cracked the door open.

"Chase, Mr. Morrison has left for the day." As she pushed the door open, a pair of feminine legs came into view. Someone was sitting in the guest chair. "Oh, I'm sorry."

Alexis Brandt was back for her Friday-night pickup.

"It's all right, Natalie." Clearly distracted, Chase looked up from some papers on his desk. He held out a set of keys. "Let me know if you need anything."

She nodded to Chase, took the keys and pulled the door closed. Her chest had tightened, and she could barely breathe. She walked on wooden legs back to Mr. Morrison's door. Her hands shook as she inserted the keys to find the right one.

She had no reason to feel jealous. She didn't have any claim to Chase—just because he'd kissed her last night didn't mean anything.

Hadn't he said that? The keys made a heavy thud when they slipped from her hands.

Squatting, she picked them up and shoved her glasses back up her nose. She was being ridiculous. Guys like Chase went for girls like Alexis. Just because he'd kissed her didn't mean he felt anything for her. He kissed women as a career. Maybe he'd just been practicing.

She found the right key and pushed into the office. Get what she needed and get out. The sooner she was done, the sooner she could be away from Chase for a whole weekend. A weekend to strengthen her resolve to stay away from him.

Papers covered Mr. Morrison's desk. Boxes of files covered the floor in front of five gray filing cabinets. This was going to take hours. Natalie shoved the keys into her jacket pocket.

Picking a drawer, she started methodically rummaging through the files. She was so absorbed in the files she tuned out the noises from down the hall. She didn't care what those two were doing, anyway. It wasn't any of her business.

After an hour she stretched, trying to loosen her muscles before heading out to her desk.

There had to be a better way. She keyed in her password but didn't have access to the reports she wanted.

Chase would have the access she needed. Her face grew warm. She didn't want to interrupt whatever was happening with Alexis.

But this would go a lot faster if she could look at the information in the computer first. If they were waiting for her to finish, this would get them out the door faster, too.

Smiling, she stood and headed down the hall. She stopped when she noticed his office door was open. He wasn't behind his desk. Had he left? Usually he stayed until she was finished, but it wasn't unfathomable that he'd left because he had better things to do than wait for her.

"Did you need something?" His voice came from behind her.

She spun on her heel. "I thought you'd left."

"I was just walking Alexis to her car. Didn't you hear us pass by the office?" He smiled, and his gaze roamed over her.

"I was working." Her words came out breathy. She cleared her throat and tried to tame the desire surging through her as his eyes settled on her lips.

Breaking eye contact, he walked around her into his office. "Have you found anything?"

Natalie took in a deep breath. She could do this. She could ignore this attraction and focus on work. She followed him into his office. "Do you have complete access to the computer system?"

"I should. What do we need to look up?" He opened his laptop, logged in and looked up at her, expectantly.

She stepped around the desk to stand behind him. Trying to ignore the smell of him, she leaned down to focus on the screen. She pointed to the icon of the reporting system. "Click there."

He followed her instructions until the report she was looking for came up.

"Can you print that out?"

"Sure. Is there anything else?" He leaned back, and his shoulder brushed her hip. She nearly leapt out of her skin. She'd been so focused on the computer. She hadn't realized she'd gotten so close to him.

"Um." She stepped back.

His chair swiveled toward her. "Natalie, it's okay." His eyes sparkled like emeralds. "People touch all the time in business. It doesn't mean anything."

Unfortunately, no one told her body that. Every touch catapulted her rational thoughts out the window, leaving her a pool of desire. Just because he didn't feel it, didn't mean she could stop.

"Of course." Warmth surged to her cheeks

as she realized she'd pressed herself against the wall as far from him as possible. Forcing herself to relax, she stepped forward again.

"Is there anything else I can do for you?" His voice had a husky quality to it, but she ignored the corresponding push from her insides.

"Bank account statements. Do you know where they would be in Mr. Morrison's office?"

He stood and she resisted the impulse to step back, but she couldn't control the wince at the expected contact. When he didn't brush against her, she raised her gaze to his face.

"I'll show you."

She couldn't breathe, let alone move. What was he going to show her? Heat poured off his body, infusing her with a drowsy feeling. Her body wanted to sway into his to see if the heat would explode into flames.

"Natalie?"

"Hmm."

"Martin's office?"

"Oh, yeah. Sorry." She turned and caught herself before she stumbled. He didn't touch her, but she could feel him directly behind her, ready to help if needed. Straightening, she walked down the hall before him, silently chastising herself.

"Here, I'll show you the drawer," Chase said.

What was she doing here with this man? He was supposed to be condescending and over-bearing. He'd been raised to be a Hollywood star, a highly publicized birth followed by a childhood in the limelight. Speculations about what features he'd get from each of his beyond-gorgeous parents had been rampant.

Critically acclaimed performances had shot him beyond the shadows of his famous par-ents. He'd taken on risky performances and made them his own. Now he was kneeling in front of a filing cabinet, rooting through bank statements.

And all she could think about was how soft

his lips had been, how he'd tasted like a hint of mint and how his body had melded against hers. Why had she let his warm eyes and smooth words convince her she could work with him? She would die a little every time someone like Alexis strutted down the hallway to his office.

She was halfway in love with this man, and if she stayed much longer, she could find herself hopelessly in love with him. Someone like him could never love someone like her. A burning sensation formed at the back of her eyes.

"Found it." Looking at the papers in the folder he was holding, he stood and walked toward her. "All the bank statements are in here. This should have the information you need."

When he met her eyes, he froze. A moment of panic flashed over his face and flowed into resignation.

"I'll come back in tomorrow to finish up." She managed to speak without a single hitch.

Even though her heart ached and she could barely breathe. She dug the keys out of her pocket and held them out to him.

"Nata—"

"Please. Don't. I can't." She turned and ran out the door.

Chapter Nine

The rain started as soon as Natalie pulled out of the parking lot. Chase stood in the doorway and watched her drive away.

He'd let her go for the good of the company. He'd done the right thing.

He set the folder with the bank statements back on her desk and closed and locked Martin's door. Her usually neat desk looked like a tornado had hit it. Every night before she left she straightened the piles. Tonight she couldn't get away fast enough and had almost left her purse behind.

Maybe he should ask Robert to come in tomorrow to help her out. His chest felt hollow. While he'd promised to back off, he couldn't resist seeing her. He just wanted to be around her, smell her sweetness, touch her soft skin. Feel like he'd finally found something real.

She could never fit into his world. She'd crumble under the pressure. He'd lose her before he ever had her, so he went back to his office and turned off the computer and lights. On his way past her desk, he noticed something sparkling under her desk.

A cell phone lay on the floor under her desk where her purse usually was. He picked it up and flipped it open. The display showed a field of flowers and her name.

He slid it into his pocket, knowing it was the wrong thing to do, but the crushing weight on his chest lifted as he opened Martin's office again. This time to get Natalie's address.

The ice cream box was almost empty by the time the movie was at the halfway point. Elizabeth was telling Chase's character, Tom, how they were meant to be together, but Tom was blowing her off, even though he loved her. Usually Natalie didn't require a tissue box and way too much Chunky Monkey ice cream to get through her favorite film. But with every close-up of Chase's face, she helped herself to a huge bite of ice cream.

It didn't help that she'd become way too familiar with his face. Seeing the expressions he'd given her on the television made her pulse pound and her heart ache.

She'd cleaned the kitchen with a vengeance first thing when she got home. Then she'd changed into her comfiest pair of jammies and popped on *If Only*. She hadn't bothered with dinner, figuring she'd get enough calories from the ice cream.

Now tucked under her blanket, she began questioning her sanity for picking the movie she'd always loved in the past. It only served to remind her of Chase's larger-than-life world. That, coupled with the magazine Rachel had left open to pictures of Chase and Alexis last weekend. Natalie wondered what else she could do to sink the dagger further into her heart.

She tried to find comfort by reminding herself she wouldn't be able to handle watching him kiss other women onscreen if he were hers. She sighed. If he were hers… The words burned in her heart. A wish that could never come true, no matter how many stars she wished upon.

Besides, she wasn't ready for a man in her life. She'd been down that road in college, and it had always ended up with her hurt and crying on Rachel's shoulder. She needed to focus on her career and worry about guys later.

Chase flashed back on the screen.

She'd have to see him in the morning. She had to finish the work before Monday. He'd said he'd be there as early as she wanted. If she could get some sleep, she might be able to deal with him in the morning.

She didn't move from the couch. She was wide awake, and though the movie made her sink further into misery, it was noise. She didn't want to fantasize about emerald eyes that burned with desire and blond hair that would be silky to the touch. She didn't want to run out to the store and find the cologne he used and wear it. She probably couldn't afford it anyway.

She shut her eyes as his image came back on the screen.

"How do you know?" his character said to Elizabeth. "How can anyone know?" His voice trickled down her spine.

She opened her eyes to see him lift his hand and caress Elizabeth's face. She imagined

Chase's hand against her cheek. He didn't kiss Elizabeth in this scene. The only kiss was the one at the end of the movie. Natalie couldn't skip to the end. What made that kiss was the journey, the tangle of emotions that preceded it and made it the most beautiful kiss she'd ever seen.

A knock at the door startled her out of the movie. She hit Pause on the remote. Who would be knocking on the door at eleven on a Friday night? She grabbed the aluminum bat they kept near the door and opened the peephole.

The night was dark and rainy. Chase stood in front of her door, dripping wet. The bat slipped from her grip, and she yanked the door open.

"What are you doing here?"

His hair was plastered to his head. Rivers of rain flowed down his face and over his grin. "Can I drip on your floor?"

She nodded, still stunned by his appearance on her doorstep, and stepped back to let him in.

She closed the door and locked it automatically. Leaning against the door, she stared at him.

He smiled down at her. "I don't suppose I could use a towel?"

"Uh, yeah. Just a moment." She walked around him into the bathroom. Her brain couldn't wrap around the fact that Chase was in her home. It was almost as if she'd conjured him from the movie. She grabbed two towels and headed out to the hallway again. He'd removed his shoes and put them on the mat near the door.

She held the towels out at arm's length for him.

"Pink. Nice."

After he took them, she wrapped her arms around her middle, suddenly vulnerable in her own home. This wasn't the office or a public restaurant, and she was in pajamas. She wondered if her overactive imagination had brought him here somehow.

He rubbed the towel over his head, leaving

his hair sticking up. Feeling her fingers tingle, she wanted to run her hands over his hair and smooth it back down.

"Was there something you needed?" she bit out, having a hard time forgetting her fantasies of him, now that the reality of him stood before her. Her body throbbed with unfulfilled desire.

He shouldered off his jacket and hung it on the doorknob. His shirt wasn't quite as wet so it didn't cling to the muscles hiding underneath, but she'd already seen that part of the movie and knew how sleek and rippled his body was under that dark shirt.

After he dried off, he reached into a coat pocket and pulled out her cell phone. "I found this in the office."

"You didn't have to bring this to me. I could have gotten it tomorrow." Wishing she'd brought the ice cream to the door with her, she reached out her hand for the phone.

When Chase lifted his gaze to hers, she

inhaled. A thousand curses on the writer of *If Only*. A thousand curses on the director, who'd decided on those scenes. She'd seen that look before. The reason she watched *If Only* a million times was because of that look. But Chase was more than his performance, he was real and thoughtful and that scared her more than the desire racing through her.

"I should go." He pressed the phone in her hand. His touch coursed through her, and he didn't lift his hand from hers.

She couldn't think as desire swelled within her. Nothing she'd experienced before compared to what Chase was making her feel. Her heart fluttered against the cage of her chest.

He closed the distance between them slightly. "I should go." His voice low and his eyes hooded.

She nodded slightly, not trusting her voice, not really meaning it. She didn't want him to go. His presence filled her vision. Her body shook with the need to be touched, but he was still holding back.

His hand slid off hers, leaving the phone in her palm. A heartbeat separated them. Much as she wanted to, Natalie couldn't drop her gaze from his. Never would she imagine Chase Booker looking at her this way. Never could she imagine Chase Booker being in her apartment. She could imagine losing her heart to him.

Not because of the fabulous roles he played, but because of who he was. She didn't see Tom from *If Only* in front of her. She saw the man who said he liked her smile. The man who picked up her glasses. The man who looked at her as if she were the only woman in the world.

She saw Chase. Her hand shook as she set the phone on the counter next to her. Risking everything for that look, she lifted her hand slowly. Her shaking fingertips traced the rough scruff along his chin.

His eyes sparked with her touch, but he didn't close the last bit of distance between them. Her fingers wandered up into his slightly damp hair. She rubbed the strands between her fingers. So soft.

"Natalie."

She pulled her gaze from his hair and met his eyes. She didn't care why he was here, just that he was here. With her. Seeing her. Making her feel beautiful.

His eyes shut, and he leaned into her hand for a moment. When he opened them, they were filled with regret. Covering her hand with his, he smiled softly. "I should go. We…we're not from the same world."

The little piece of hope that had flared to life went out. Not from the same world. He was Mr. Popularity and she was the nerd. That may not be what he meant, but that's how it felt.

She slid her hand out from under his. His hand clung to hers until it was freed. He flexed his fingers as he dropped his hand to his side.

He wasn't unaffected by her, but she wasn't enough to tempt him to stay.

His fingers lifted her chin until she met his eyes again. "I…" He dropped his hand. "I've got to go."

Turning, he shrugged on his coat and stepped into his shoes. She leaned against the wall for support. She had nothing to add. She couldn't have spoken if she wanted to.

He didn't look at her as he struggled with the locks and the doorknob. Stepping forward, she brushed his hands aside, undid the locks and pulled the door open. The scent of rain, fresh and clean, filled the small space.

He stepped out. "I'll see you in the morning."

"Yeah," she rasped as she eased the door shut. Before it closed fully, it stopped.

Natalie stepped back from the door as it slowly opened.

Chase stood in the doorway, hands braced on the door frame. Rain coursed over him.

His head hung down. His fingers curved into the wood as if some invisible wall separated them.

"Natalie, tell me to leave and I will." Haunted green eyes rose to meet her eyes. "I don't want to leave, but if you tell me to, I will."

Her heart struggled against her chest. "I…" She dropped her gaze to the puddle forming at his feet. What would it mean if she let Chase in again? Would they make love and then just forget about each other? Would it be enough?

"Natalie?"

She lifted her gaze to his. Could she resist this opportunity? Did she want to? God yes, she wanted him. She clamped her lips together to stop her doubts from emerging and held out her hand.

He dropped his head again before pushing off the door frame and into the apartment. "To hell with right and wrong." His foot kicked the door shut as his hand closed over hers.

He yanked her into his arms, and his mouth

crashed down on hers. Her jammies were soaked within seconds but she didn't care. A flood of desire pooled in her core, and her body tingled where his warmth radiated through his clothes.

The intensity of his kiss thrilled her down to her toes. He lifted her against him. His arousal pressed into her stomach as an answering pulse surged between her thighs. A sensuous fog of lust clouded her mind as his mouth trailed away to her neck. Her feet met the floor again and he released her. She whimpered.

He smiled as he kicked off his shoes and dropped his jacket on the floor. He closed the distance between their bodies and tipped up her face to his. His mouth stopped above hers, and his eyes delved into hers. "I couldn't leave you now. I need you, Natalie. You. Only you."

His mouth pressed against hers. Her hands sank into his wet locks and held him there. She wanted this moment more than she wanted to breathe. He gathered her in his arms and worked her backward down the hall.

His head lifted and his forehead rested against hers as they both gulped down air. His heart raced against hers. "Which way do we go?"

She opened her eyes to his deep green ones. His hand brushed over the back of her neck, and her eyelids slid shut. His chest rubbed against her breasts. Her lips parted. Had he asked something?

Her eyelids lifted. His eyes smiled down at her.

"Don't you have a roommate?" His voice was husky and deep. It sent shivers down her spine.

"Rachel?"

"Much as I love the camera, I don't want to put on a show tonight. I want you all to myself." His fingertip traced the curve of her ear.

"Oh." His words penetrated the fog invading her mind. "She's out tonight." The smell of rain and his woodsy scent overwhelmed her nose. It coursed down her body to settle in her belly.

"Where's your room, Natalie?" His teeth nipped the tender skin of her jaw, and her pulse leapt. The desire reflected in his gaze finally broke through the fog.

She turned within his arms. His hand lifted her hair from her neck, and his mouth caressed the back of her neck. If his arm hadn't been around her, she would have melted into a puddle at his feet.

"Room?" His warm breath fanned the nape of her neck.

Right, room. She led him into the living room. He'd mercifully lifted his head from his torment of her neck, giving her some space to think. His arm remained around her waist. The backs of his fingers skimmed down the side of her breast.

She stopped in her tracks. Her breath caught in her throat at the whisper of a touch, and she leaned back into the warmth of his chest. A drop of water splattered on her forehead.

His finger brushed away the drop. "I could use another towel."

This was really happening. Chase was in her living room, touching and kissing her. Not just in her mind or on the screen. Screen? Her gaze darted to the TV still paused on Chase's face.

The red-hot lava of embarrassment filled her cheeks even as pools of liquid fire gathered between her thighs and his mouth worked down the side of her neck again. Maybe he wouldn't notice.

"Not the best still frame, but definitely a good scene." His breath was hot against her neck as he spoke.

So much for hoping he wouldn't notice. Normally, she'd wish for the floor to swallow her whole, but she didn't want to be out of Chase's arms for one second. "I think that's one of your best smiles."

His mouth curved into a smile as he dropped a kiss on her lips.

"I stand corrected," Natalie said as she struggled to control her breathing. "That is your best smile."

He leaned down until his lips were next to her ear. "You ain't seen nothing yet."

His hand trailed from her waist to cup her breast. Her nipples hardened, and she fought to control her breathing. His body was hard against her back. She completely forgot the TV as urgency filled her. Her body pulsed.

His thumb stroked her nipple through her damp pajama top. His other hand relinquished her hip and worked on the buttons of her top. Her hands found his hips, something solid to cling to as desire pulled her farther down. When the top few buttons were undone, his hand slipped inside. His flesh brushed against her nipple. Warmth pooled between her legs.

"Natalie." Her name was a growl upon his lips.

Her shirt fell open when he finished with the buttons. His hands brushed the shirt down her arms and it slid to the floor. His mouth caressed the sensitive area between her neck and her shoulder.

His hands stroked back up her arms. She was beyond lost. Any doubts she may have felt went up in smoke. She turned in his arms.

Looking down into liquid pools of chocolate, Chase shuddered at the trust and longing revealed there. Gently he removed her glasses and set them on the table next to him. Unable to resist the parting of her lips, he lowered his mouth to hers, taking his time to savor the sweet taste of her.

He lifted his head and yanked his shirt over his head. Pulling her tight against his chest, he rejoiced in the feeling of her flesh sliding against his, but it wasn't enough.

His hands smoothed over her back down to

the waistband of her pajamas. They were hardly the sexy lingerie he'd had the pleasure to see and remove, but somehow the tiny kitten print on cotton suited Natalie.

She rested her head against his hammering heart. Her hands wrapped around his back. Her fingers were tentative on the top of his jeans, but her touch left a trail of fire. Damn it, he wanted to get her to a bed. He wanted to be everything she desired, but she didn't seem to care where they were, which enflamed his desire for her more.

His hands slipped below her waistband, curving over her bottom and pulling her tight against his arousal. Her fingernails scraped his lower back, and a shiver rippled down his spine.

Her fingers found their way below his waistband. Unable to deny himself any longer, he held her shoulders to push her away. She gazed up at him as he lifted her to meet his mouth. Her legs wrapped around his waist.

The center of her rubbed intimately against his arousal as his mouth caressed hers. His tongue touched her lips and she opened them, greeting his tongue with hers.

Natalie felt as if she were falling as his shoulders bunched under her fingers. As he lowered her to the floor, his smooth skin warmed under her touch. The carpeting brushed her back, and he settled on top of her.

His mouth never left hers as his hands returned to her waist. Pushing her bottoms off, he broke contact briefly before returning to her lips. Maybe he was worried that she'd change her mind, but she couldn't stop this. Her hands brushed over his back to convince herself he was here and not just a dream from sugar overload.

She reached for the buttons on his jeans. His chest brushed her tender nipples as he pushed off his pants. He reached into his pocket to pull out a condom before flinging his pants away.

His flesh warm against hers. Her body ready

and aching to know the feel of his. His hands lifted her hips. As his mouth ravished hers, his erection pressed against her opening.

This was real. She was awake, and it was really happening. Chase was with her.

Instinctively, her hips rocked against him, longing to draw him in. He lifted his mouth from hers and held still.

"Open your eyes, Natalie." His voice was on the edge of control and the complete loss of control.

Her eyes met his and he buried himself in her. Her lips parted at the sensations pulsing within her. Again he waited until her eyes met his before he began to move within her.

His eyes held hers as the pressure within her boiled to the breaking point. The intimacy of watching his eyes filled with want and restraint pushed her over the edge. Her eyelids fluttered as she peaked, free-falling into the abyss. But she kept her eyes open and locked with his.

When she began to relax, he moved within

her again. Sparking her sensitive flesh into a renewed fever, she gripped his shoulders and they surged together. His forehead rested against hers as his body tensed and released.

She relished the weight of him against her as he relaxed over her. Her mind was a jumbled mess, but she knew it wouldn't last. She'd just slept with Chase Booker, become another notch on his bedpost. Had the most intense orgasm of her life.

She closed her eyes.

Her arms and legs were wrapped around his sweat-slick body. He covered every inch of her. She didn't want to move, but she could barely breathe. Holy crap, she'd had sex with Chase Booker.

Chase lifted his weight on his forearms and looked down into Natalie's eyes. His heart swelled in his chest at the shy smile she gave him. "So which one was your bedroom?"

Her head rolled to the side, and she pointed

to one of the doors. "That one, I think." She squinted "It's a bit blurry at the moment."

He sat up and reached over onto the table where he'd set her glasses. He stretched out beside her and lowered her glasses to her face. The blush that usually disappeared into her blouse's neckline spread over the tops of her breasts.

Unable to resist, he trailed his finger where the blush faded into pale skin. Her skin reddened even further. Her hand reached up to the blanket on the couch, but he caught her wrist.

"Don't. I like looking at you."

Her hand curled into a fist, but she made no move to cover herself. Even though she was short, her body was well proportioned. Her breasts were small and unaltered. They were perfect. He traced his fingertip over the tip. The nipple puckered under his touch.

"Shouldn't we go to the bedroom? Or turn off a light?" Maybe he'd be willing to let her light a candle instead of having lamps on. He seemed mesmerized as his fingers trailed lower. Over her slightly rounded belly, his finger left a line of fire in its wake. The fire shot straight to her core, building her arousal again.

They'd had sex in her living room. On the floor. She closed her eyes as embarrassment warred with desire. She wanted him to stop so they could cover up somehow, but she didn't want him to stop what he was doing.

His hand flattened on her stomach, and she inhaled deeply of his cologne, the rain, him. Her belly quivered as his hand dipped lower until his fingertips slipped between her thighs.

Her breath hissed out between her teeth. His lips touched hers as his fingers gently moved over and in her. His tongue traced her lower lip as his finger circled her sex. Her fingers sank into the carpet as her body arched into his palm. Her side pressed into his warm, hard muscles.

When he removed his hand, she whimpered with need. The condom package rustled. He covered her with his body and entered her smoothly. Her body buzzed with pent-up frustration, and her desire soared as she crested the edge again. His climax followed close behind hers, and he collapsed against her.

She had the overwhelming urge to laugh. Her body had always been wound so tight, and now she felt as if the spring had finally broken. Her limbs were like water. She'd never been so satisfied in her life.

When he raised his head and peered into her eyes, her breath caught. Her heart flipped, and she knew she was in trouble.

Chapter Ten

Light peeked through the slightly parted curtain to torment Natalie. She squeezed her eyes shut and rolled straight into a solid, warm object. A very naked solid, warm object whose very naked arm was wrapped around her very naked body.

Cracking open her eyes, she stared at the slightly blurry image of Chase. His chest rose and fell gently. Her hand rested on his well-formed abs underneath her lavender sheets.

Her body ached pleasantly, and she smiled

as she recalled gathering up the clothes strewn across the apartment and managing to make it to the bed for round three. Her comforter was half off the bed and pillows were scattered throughout the room.

She rested her cheek against his chest and listened to the rhythmic pace of his heart. She wished the sun would go away and leave her forever in the night with Chase. Morning meant responsibility. Morning meant work. Morning meant regret.

As she snuggled against him, she wondered if he'd regret last night. She couldn't. Chase had wanted her. It still seemed unfathomable, but he wanted her.

His chest shifted under her, and his fingers lightly brushed down her hair. "Good morning." His voice was satisfied and low. His lips touched her forehead.

"Morning." Should she add more? What were the expectations when someone woke in the arms of the Sexiest Man Alive? But that's not who she'd been with last night. She'd been with Chase, just Chase. The suave heartthrob from the screen had disappeared, leaving behind the man who made her feel beautiful. Who cared enough to give her a choice. Who was flesh and blood, not just a character on a show.

His arm tightened around her waist. "Relax. Everything will be fine." His heartbeat increased under her ear, and she felt his growing arousal next to her thigh.

"We should get to work," she whispered. Her sore body flooded with heat.

His hand slipped down to cup one of her breasts. "You're right. We should." His other hand reached over to the nightstand for a condom.

She gasped as he shifted her on top of him. His full arousal rested against the junction of her legs. "Chase." His name came out on a breath as she lowered her hips to meet his.

They came together slowly. Bodies sliding

against each other. His hands controlled the pace of her hips. Her core rippled with each slow withdrawal and excruciating slow return. Her mind melted with the fire of her arousal until she lived for the next caress, the next brush, the next penetration.

As she found climax, she arched and cried out. He sat up with her, drawing her body against his, and continued to raise and lower her hips until his climax took him. They fell back to the bed. Her thighs trembled as she lay on top of him.

She couldn't remember a time she'd been so thoroughly sated. Her breathing returned to normal, and her heart slowed its frantic beat. It was time to get back to the real world, where he was larger than life, and she was happy being a flower on the wall.

Natalie sat on the floor of Mr. Morrison's office surrounded by files. She stared out the window as her mind wandered back to the care and tenderness Chase had shown when they'd shared the shower. She'd been beet-red the entire time, but she'd enjoyed every moment.

They'd managed to get out of the apartment before Rachel came in, which had Natalie counting her blessings. Meeting Chase in the office was one thing, but finding he'd spent the night with Natalie would definitely blow Rachel's mind.

Now, he sat down the hall in his office, while she picked through files. When she could get her mind to focus on them. Every time she heard a sound she'd jump. She didn't think Mr. Morrison worked on the weekends, but she knew her luck couldn't hold out. Then there was Chase. She just didn't know what to expect or how to react to him today.

She'd been a permanent shade of pink this morning. He didn't seem to want to let her out of his sight, though he did allow her some privacy in the bathroom. She'd also convinced him to let her drive her car instead of riding with him.

The kiss he'd given her before they left the apartment had ricocheted through her sore body. He didn't just kiss with his mouth. He kissed with his whole body, drawing her so close.

She'd sagged against her car waiting for him to get in his, before shaking herself. Time to get on with it. Maybe she was just a fascination. Something different from what he usually went after. He'd cast her aside when a shiny new something passed by.

She returned her attention to the file in her lap. Whatever it was between them, it couldn't last. Maybe she should end it now before she got too hurt. She rubbed the ache that began in her chest at the thought. Yeah, it was definitely too late to avoid pain, but she did enjoy the pleasure.

Chase stood in the doorway of Martin's office and took in his little accountant surrounded by mounds of paper, an expression of intensity on her face. A soft smile teased the corner of her lips. He'd put that there.

He wanted to see where this thing between them could go, but the moment the press got ahold of it they'd latch on and shake it until it broke. He could protect her from that, if they were careful. Maybe this hadn't been his best idea—the press was already sniffing around because of the breakup, and he needed the publicity for his upcoming film.

His thoughts flew out the window when she turned her face up to him and that crimson flush covered her cheeks. For a moment, he allowed himself to sink into her wide eyes and feel the wholesomeness of her. Her lips parted in a silent invitation he wasn't sure she was aware of.

He cleared his throat. "How's it going?"

Her eyes wandered over the folders. "I don't think I'm going to be able to get through this today. I need more time."

He longed to smooth his fingers over the creases in her forehead. "I think we can put Martin off for a few days, while you continue to investigate. You give him a report that doesn't mention the expenses. Everything matched up, right? Receipts and expenses are all accounted for?"

"Yes, there are forms for everything, but when will I be able to work on it with him being here during the day?" Frustration poured off her.

He leaned against the doorway. "We'll stay late and go through it together. I always thought Martin was a good man and want to make absolutely sure before I accuse him of anything."

Her gaze flitted up to his. Her eyes spoke volumes as worry, fear and desire whipped through them. What did she fear? Him? "Together," she said, resigned.

"Let's clean up this mess and get out of here. We could pick up some takeout and go back to my place?" Suddenly, he was nervous, like a boy asking a girl out for the first time. After last night that was a ridiculous thought, but it was there, a tingle of anticipation and fear of rejection.

If he ended it now, they wouldn't have to worry about the press. No one would ever find out, and Natalie would stay happy in her simple life. And he'd go back to dating the same women he'd always dated. But what if this was the only shot he had at something real?

She started stacking the files without looking up at him. "Do you think we should?" Her hands trembled as she set the papers down. "I mean, don't you have plans with Alexis? It is Saturday night."

He knelt beside her and used his finger under her chin to turn her face to his. A sadness lingered in her eyes. "The only person I want to be with tonight is right here." He traced her lower lip with his thumb. "Please say yes."

The warring factions continued for a moment

within her eyes. Her face flushed, and her shy smile appeared, easing the tightness in his chest. "Yes."

Chase's house was bigger than Natalie had imagined. He lived in Hollywood Hills with the A-list celebrities. The houses lining the streets weren't simple homes, but complexes with long, gated drives.

She followed in her car up the drive and around to the back of the house. Two garage doors opened along the huge building. She pulled her Honda Fit in next to an expensive-looking silver car.

The garage door closed behind her. She stepped out into a huge room with a high ceiling and painted concrete floors. A couple of the cars had shrouds over them, but she could tell by the shape that they were sport cars.

She'd been happy when she'd qualified for the loan on her Fit, which she would pay off in five years. She highly doubted there were loans on the six cars in this garage. Each one was probably at least five times the new price of hers.

Chase strode to her side. "Do you like cars?"

"Um, well, they get me from here to there, but not really." She was lucky to have the old beater that got her through college. She hadn't needed a car before that, since her mother had homeschooled her.

His fingers laced into hers. "C'mon. Let me show you my house."

She tried to ignore the fizzle of awareness that coursed through her at his touch. His grip was strong and gentle as he pulled her through the door connecting the house to the garage.

The kitchen was enormous. Cream-colored tile swept across the floor. Dark wood cabinets and sparkling stainless steel appliances filled one end of the kitchen, while the other end had floor-to-ceiling windows and a simple kitchen table with chairs.

Chase set the bags of food down on the table and tugged her into his arms. Kissing him was like kissing an electrical socket. Her whole body sparked to life, aware of every inch of him pressed against every inch of her. His hand loosened the knot in her hair before cradling her head.

When he came up for air, she could barely stand. Her knees turned to jelly, and her core pulsed with need.

"Welcome to my home." He smiled down at her and kissed the tip of her nose.

"Is that always part of the welcome?" She held on to his arms to brace herself.

"For you, it should be." His smile was warm as he set her aside. "Now, if you'll stop groping me—"

"I'm not the one grop—"

He brushed his lips over hers. "We can eat. Then I can show you around." With his hand on her lower back, he guided her to one of the chairs surrounding the cherrywood table. He moved around the kitchen efficiently.

"Do you cook?" Natalie asked.

When he returned, he set the table with china, silverware and wine glasses. "I get by. My housekeeper keeps the kitchen stocked with essentials. I like to cook and don't always order out if that's what you're asking." He winked before heading to the fridge.

"It's just…I suppose I thought…"

He uncorked a bottle of white wine.

"You thought that I wouldn't want to?" he offered. As he sat, his thigh brushed hers, sending little ripples of desire racing through her. His eyes danced.

"Maybe." She couldn't think much of anything when he was near.

After he poured the wine, he pulled out a couple of containers. "I hope you like La Bouche Paisible." His hand brushed hers as she took the glass.

"I've never eaten there before." She didn't

think her paycheck would cover the dinner. Not to mention she'd need something better to wear than her current wardrobe could provide to get in the door. She shoved her glasses up her nose, wishing her contacts would magically appear.

"Well, you are in for an experience."

She was already having an experience that was beyond belief. And she was more than willing to follow this golden brick road until she found her way back home.

After he dished out the contents of the containers, there was still one left.

"What's that?"

He smiled mysteriously. "Dessert."

Her plate overflowed with food. A filet steak with brown gravy, new potatoes with herbs, grilled asparagus and the scent—her stomach rumbled from the delicious smells emanating from her plate.

"Where'd you grow up?" he asked before taking a bite of steak.

"What makes you think I'm not from here?" she asked, trying to sound serious.

His eyebrow lifted, causing her to laugh.

"I'm from the Midwest. Illinois. We moved out to California my senior year when dad got a transfer. I've been here ever since."

"Do you see your family much?"

"No, my older sister stayed in Illinois when we moved, and Dad got transferred again while I was in college. We see each other at holidays, of course." Natalie bit into the steak and her mouth exploded with flavor. "Oh, wow."

He smiled, pleased with himself. "Yeah."

After she swallowed the small piece of heaven, she turned to him. "What about you?"

"For the most part, my birth and subsequent childhood are public record."

"Assume I don't know anything, because I wasn't around when you were born." She wanted to know how he felt about growing up with his family, not what the press reported.

"Well, I spent a lot of my time on movie sets or in foreign countries. I had a tutor and a nanny. My parents tried to keep me out of the tabloids, but when I started auditioning all bets were off."

"How old were you?" she asked gently.

"I was eight." He set down his fork and picked up his wineglass. Staring at the contents, he continued, "I was ten when I had my first crush. She was an actress, too. We made it into all the teeny-bop magazines."

"I never read any of those."

His gaze pivoted to her and gave her an assessing look. "I don't suppose you would have. When it ended, I talked to my parents about going to a real high school. After all, I'd played a high schooler on TV, how hard could real life be?"

"I never went to high school. Mom homeschooled me, but I bet you were the coolest kid in school." She pushed her plate away and picked up her wineglass.

His hand covered hers on the table. "Not really. Sure, I had all the toys boys like and the best clothes, but I'd never really socialized with kids my own age before." He picked up her hand and turned it over. His finger traced the lines on her palm. "I found a group and dated a little, but they either resented me for who I was or wanted something from me."

Something troubled him, but she didn't press. The more she learned about him the more real he seemed. The harder it would be to let him go.

He pushed back from the table. "Come on. I want to show you my home. I'll bring dessert."

He grabbed a couple of spoons and the container before taking her hand and leading her across the kitchen.

The rest of his house was as amazing and intimidating as the kitchen. From the crystal chandeliers in the dining room to the antiques in the living room. From the extra-large-screen

TV in the media room to the red-lined pool table in the recreation room. The splendor and richness made her head spin.

"How long have you lived here?" She knew the man was a multimillionaire. She knew he wore expensive clothes, even if they were casual, but it hadn't really hit her. Now it slapped her across the face. Her apartment could fit into his media room.

"This was my parents' home. I inherited it." He seemed to choke up on the statement before it passed. "Besides, it's small compared to the one I own in Italy."

Her head still reeling, he opened a door and pulled her into a darkened room. She slammed into his back as he halted and flipped a switch. Soft lights lit the interior of the room.

She stepped around Chase and her mouth dropped open. Before her, tropical trees and flowers filled the room in bold colors, reds, yellows, greens and blues. The scent of the flowers and the leafy smell of the trees perfumed the air. A glass roof and walls enclosed the garden.

A stone path wound its way along the floor through the trees and disappeared into the foliage. She could hear the chirps of birds somewhere in the room.

"My favorite room." Chase's hand rested at her lower back.

"I can see why." She gaped up at the large, colorful flowers as he led her farther into the room. The back was blocked off and filled with tropical birds of all colors. She stopped as a large toucan swept down to the ground where a bowl of fruit rested near a small pond. It was unbelievable. Almost like stepping through a doorway onto a tropical island.

"Here we are." He led her into a small gazebo open to the sights and sounds of the room, but secluded from the door to the rest of the house.

"You could forget where you are in here." She

settled on the pillows covering the floor, still trying to absorb all the colors and scents.

"That's the point. I can't always make time to escape to a tropical location, but I can usually slip into this room. I'm pretty good at pretending." He lowered himself down beside her and stretched out on his side. "Dessert?"

Tearing her gaze from a beautiful orange flower, she found herself captivated by his eyes, and her breathing hitched.

She knew why she'd agreed to come here to his house.

She wasn't strong enough to walk away from Chase. She didn't want to walk away from the attraction between them. When it was over, she was fairly certain it would be him doing the walking.

But that didn't mean she couldn't enjoy the ride. "What did you have in mind?"

His grin was positively wicked. He popped the lid off the last container. "Dark chocolate mousse."

He handed her a spoon and dug his into the creamy mousse. He lifted the spoon to her mouth and waited.

Her gaze never left his as she leaned forward and took the spoon and chocolate into her mouth. The sweetness and the slight bitterness of the chocolate combined to form ecstasy in her mouth. She closed her eyes and savored the taste rolling around on her tongue.

Before she could open her eyes, soft lips pressed against hers. His mouth tasted like the wine they'd been drinking flavored with the chocolate of the mousse. She didn't resist when his body shifted, pushing her back into the pillows.

His hands lifted her glasses from her face before his mouth returned to the gentle assault on her senses. She'd never experienced anything quite like Chase before. Every opportunity he could touch her, he did. Every chance to kiss her, he took.

As his lips caressed her neck, she wondered

if this wasn't a good idea. "Maybe…maybe we should stop." Her fingers dug into his shoulders as he sucked her earlobe into his mouth.

"Mmm-hmm. You're right. We haven't finished dessert yet." His mouth returned to hers. His tongue slid along her bottom lip. His hands caressed the sides of her body, pulling her firmly up into his body. Her flesh warmed beneath his, responding to his fire.

"Chase?" she murmured against his lips. He raised his head and she forgot what she was going to say at the gentle smile on his lips and the desire in his eyes. That was a look she'd never seen in his movies. Any protests she may have had died on her tongue. She hadn't really meant them anyway.

"Would you like more dessert?" His finger lightly brushed over her nipple.

A shudder coursed through her. Resistance was futile. "Yes, please."

Chapter Eleven

Sitting cross-legged on Chase's king-size bed wearing only his T-shirt, Natalie picked up one of the chocolate-covered strawberries from the tray. She couldn't wipe the ridiculously pleased smile off her face and didn't really want to.

Sunday afternoon had never been her favorite day or time. Usually it was reserved for doing laundry or running errands. But after spending the last few hours in Chase's arms, it was definitely moving to the top of her list.

Unfortunately, Monday morning would follow closely on its heels.

She glanced at the open bedroom door. Chase had discovered her weakness for sweets and had promised her the best hot chocolate ever. He'd kissed her soundly before insisting she stay in bed and conserve her energy.

She'd never felt so pampered or so thoroughly loved before. Her muscles and body ached, but it was a pleasant ache. It couldn't possibly last, though. Tomorrow was Monday, after all.

While this fantasy had been fabulous and she never wanted it to end, Monday changed everything. Back to the real world. Back to being an accountant beneath notice and an actor on the cover of *People*.

"Whoa, what happened to that smile?" Chase in only a pair of boxer briefs stood in the doorway, balancing a tray. "There it is." He set the tray on the massive nightstand and joined her on the bed. "I'm sorry to inform you that I'm out of chocolate, but I found some protein instead."

He produced a plate with a turkey sandwich cut into squares. "Eat. You need your energy."

She smiled and pushed her glasses back up her nose. "Thanks." Taking a sandwich, she smiled at him.

He lay down beside her on the bed and rubbed the hem of her shirt between two fingers. The back of his fingers brushed her skin, fanning the ever-present flame.

He helped himself to a sandwich square and a chocolate-covered strawberry. She couldn't keep her mind from their shared bath last night or the morning spent in this bed.

She picked off a corner of the sandwich and chewed it thoughtfully. "What are we going to do about tomorrow?"

He dragged his finger lazily up her leg. "What about tomorrow?" He kissed her thigh and looked up at her with his lazy grin.

Her heart leapt, and her body responded with a pulsing need. She needed to focus. "Work. Chase, stop that. We need to talk about work."

He picked up her plate and set it on the table. He handed her a bottle of water and sat up on the bed with her. "What about work?" This time his eyes were serious as he watched her drink.

She almost spilled from the intensity of his gaze. She capped the water before it ended up all over the bed.

"Well?" He took the bottle from her and set it aside.

"Well, what do we do about this?"

He scooted behind her and pulled her back to his front. She leaned her head back against him. He wrapped one arm around her shoulder and the other around her stomach, pulling her tight against him.

His voice was quiet and soft when he asked,

"What do you want?" His arms tightened around her.

She turned her head so that her cheek rested on his bare chest. His heartbeat echoed in her ears. He made her feel warm and safe and beautiful.

She sighed. She wanted to stay like this forever, but that wasn't likely to happen. A whole world waited outside those doors. "I…I don't know."

"Stay with me."

"I can't do that. What about the media?"

His cheek rested against the top of her head. "What if I weren't famous and a line of paparazzi didn't hang on my every move?" His voice had an edge to it.

"I—I don't know. I—I—" She'd almost slipped and said "love." "I like you, Chase. I like spending time with you, but this can't possibly work."

"What if we didn't go public? What if we kept this to ourselves?" It sounded reasonable, but how many other girls had thought the same thing and ended up as tabloid fodder.

"Has that ever worked? It seems like those relationships always get caught. I can't be that girl. I don't want that kind of attention."

Desperation filled her. She didn't want to stop seeing Chase, but what choice did she have? She wasn't made of the stuff needed to be a Hollywood star's girlfriend. She would be compared to all his ex-girlfriends. There was no way she could measure up against the likes of Alexis Brandt. Eventually Chase would realize the mistake he'd made by being with Natalie.

His arms squeezed her. He shifted them until she lay under him. In the move, the soft T-shirt had bunched up at her waist. He lowered his mouth to hers. Afraid this could be over, she met his lips with all the desire she felt. Her hands grabbed his head to hold it there.

His hands skimmed down her sides to her panties, and her body arched up into his erection. This could be the last time. She didn't want this to ever end.

He shifted slightly while he retrieved a condom from the nightstand, but his mouth never left hers. His teeth nipped at her lips. He slid into her as his mouth continued to devastate hers. She sighed against his lips, and her body shuddered with longing.

She'd wanted to feel this all her life. The connection, the intimacy. It swelled up within her. How could she ever let this go? But she had to—she wasn't cut out for his lifestyle.

He lifted his head and gazed down into her eyes. She needed his mouth back on hers. She needed him to move within her and take them over the edge. He was an addiction, and she just needed one more hit.

His eyes searched hers. "Don't leave."

Her core pulsed around him. "But—"

"No *buts*. We don't have to go public. I want you." The muscles in his arms shook as he held himself above her.

He moved within her slowly, maintaining eye contact. She could feel him touching her soul as he slowly drove her insane. She didn't ever want this to end.

"Natalie?"

She met his heated gaze and felt the pressure building within her.

"Stay."

Her resolve to end it now before it would hurt too much crumbled at the look in his eyes. It was going to hurt when it ended, but she couldn't bear to let go. She'd take all she could get. Her body shook with her decision. "I'll stay, Chase."

His mouth covered hers, and he thrust within her again. Her body convulsed around him as she returned his kiss. Joy filled her heart. His body arched into hers once more before he collapsed against her. Her fingers tangled in his hair as they both drifted back to themselves. Where was the harm in trying?

* * *

By Monday morning the weekend rain had passed, leaving everything greener and brighter. Natalie had gone home Sunday, and Rachel hadn't even missed her. Rachel had asked what she'd done last night, and Natalie had mentioned going out to a movie or shopping or something.

Her heart had been full, and her body had been relaxed. She'd slept wonderfully last night, with only thoughts of Chase racing through her brain.

Natalie had come in early this morning to get the report finished for Mr. Morrison. Her heart jumped every time the exterior door opened, knowing that Chase would be here soon.

When Mr. Morrison showed up at nine, Natalie had handed him the report with trembling hands, sure he would sense she knew. Mr. Morrison took it and didn't spare her another glance as he made his way back to his office.

The morning dragged on, but still no Chase.

Natalie lost herself in her work. When Mr. Morrison went out for lunch, she pulled out the copies of the bank statements and listed the cash withdrawals. She made sure they were put away before he returned.

She took a quick break to run and get something to eat at her desk. By then she figured Chase wasn't coming in. She didn't want to arouse anyone's suspicions by asking the receptionist about him. Her nervous energy drained off as she spent the afternoon engrossed in an audit of another film that Mr. Morrison wanted her to do.

"Good night, Natalie. That was a fine report you put together."

She broke away from the list of numbers she was adding to look up at Mr. Morrison blankly.

"Chase and Robert have it on their desks now. Don't worry about working late this week." Mr. Morrison locked his door and left before Natalie could think of anything to say.

Her head was spinning. Was Chase here? Why hadn't she noticed him go by? Why hadn't he said anything? She picked up her water bottle and headed down to the kitchen. She at least could check to see if his light was on.

It wasn't like they'd actually made any plans for today. Maybe he'd had time to think about it and really didn't want to be with her anymore. Maybe it'd just been a line to make her feel better. Her stomach dropped. Well, it wasn't like it was going to last.

She slowed her pace as she reached the end of the hall near his office. His door was shut, but light peeked out from under the door. Was that the sun or his desk light?

She sighed and went into the kitchen. Why did she care? They were just going to have an affair. It's not like they'd decided to date. She had been the one to try to cut things off. The water ran over the top of her bottle.

Maybe he'd decided that she was right. Her heart twisted but she ignored it. Maybe this was for the best. Not sparing his door another glance, she headed back to her desk. Putting it out of her mind, she filed what she was working on and pulled out the documents for *Night Blooming.* Chase wouldn't hide from her. Obviously, he had to do stuff away from the office sometimes.

She shoved her glasses up on her nose. She'd checked the shipping documents online for her contacts. They were supposed to be delivered today. Maybe she would call it an early night. After all, hadn't Chase said they should work on it together?

She heard the door close as the last person left. Well, she thought, the last one, except for her and potentially Chase, if he really was in his office. She sighed. She had it bad.

Her computer fan shut down, leaving the office in silence. She glanced down the hallway. She could knock to see if he was there and tell him she was leaving for the night. If he wasn't there, no one would know. If he was there…well, she could cross that bridge when it happened.

As she moved to stand, her desk phone rang. It was almost six o'clock. Who would be calling her at work?

"This is Natalie."

"Hi, Natalie. Jared Anderson. Before you hang up, let me apologize for the way I came off the other day. I'm just trying to show people the real Chase Booker."

She almost hung up the phone, but his last sentence stuck with her. "The real Chase Booker?"

"You know, the man behind the legend. The real Chase Booker, not the public persona."

Actually she was very familiar with the real Chase Booker, or at least the Chase Booker he'd shown her. How could she really trust that was the real Chase? He was a great actor. Award winning. What made her think he wasn't acting with her?

"Hello? Are you still there?" Jared's voice cut across the phone line.

She cleared her thoughts. "I'm sorry. I really can't help you."

"That's fine. I'm going to send you an e-mail with my contact info in case you change your mind. Good night, Natalie."

She hung up the phone. Maybe he was right. Maybe no one knew the real Chase. Her mind wandered back to this weekend. Her pulse kicked up a notch and she released a breath. If that hadn't been real, she didn't know what was.

Or maybe she just didn't want to know if it was faked. Maybe she wanted to cling to those feelings for a little while longer.

Chapter Twelve

Chase set down the phone. All day it had been one disaster after another. He'd avoided going anywhere near Natalie today for fear he wouldn't be able to resist pulling her into his arms.

His life had always been filled with beautiful women willing to give him anything. Whenever he was available, another woman would slide effortlessly into the role of girlfriend. Natalie's reluctance to be a part of his public life was something he'd never dealt with before. Even his high school girlfriend had loved the extra attention at first.

Everything about Natalie felt different, and he was afraid of letting her slip through his fingers. For once in his life, he wasn't sure what to do.

He'd hoped to catch her before she left for the day, but at five a director had called him to work out some issues with their next production. An hour later, he'd worked through the details, but feared Natalie had already left the office.

Pushing back from his desk, he strode to his door and yanked it open. Natalie stood there looking achingly uncertain. Her pale face bloomed red as she met his eyes.

Quickly glancing down the hall and seeing no one, he grabbed her hand and pulled her into his office. He slammed the door and slipped his arms around her, gathering her close. He lowered his head and found her lips with his. The stress of the day fell away as her arms clung to his neck, and her lips responded to his.

It'd only been a day since he'd seen her, but it felt like forever as his hands skimmed her backside. Her hands sank into his hair holding him close, but not close enough for him. He reached behind her and clicked the door lock into place before lifting her. Still rediscovering her sweet mouth, he set her on the edge of his desk. Her fingers worked on the buttons of his shirt while his worked on hers.

His hands skimmed over the satin of her chemise. The softness eased the ache within him slightly. He took a breath and smiled down at her.

"Hi." He pushed her shirt down her arms and kissed her collar bone.

"Hi."

He looked up in time to catch her smile, the one she only gave to him. Her cheeks and neck were flushed, but he knew it was due to arousal rather than embarrassment.

He smoothed his hands up her thighs, raising her skirt as he went. "I missed you last night."

She scooted forward on the desk until her body was pressed against his. "I missed you, too." Her voice trembled. "Maybe we shouldn't do this here." But she made no move to push him away.

He pressed his mouth to hers and ran his hand up her inner thighs. "Do you have someplace better in mind?"

Her sharp inhale was followed by a tightened grip on his arm. Her eyes unfocused as his hand reached the juncture of her thighs. Her lips parted.

Unable to resist, he captured her mouth as his hand slipped beneath her underwear to the warm, wet flesh beneath. He caught her gasp in his mouth.

His cell phone vibrated on the table. He ignored it, knowing it would go to voice mail, and nothing was more important than Natalie at this moment.

He pulled away from her to slide her underwear down her legs and slid off her sandals. Her hands sought his chest, his shoulders, his back. Every touch branded him as hers.

He made quick work of his jeans and a condom before drawing her into his arms. He tried to ease into her, but she linked her legs around his back and pulled him into her fully.

The air escaped his lungs at the feeling of her surrounding him, her legs around his waist, her hands on his shoulders, her breasts crushed against his chest. He withdrew and sank into her again. His lips sought hers as they came together at a frantic pace.

Had it only been a day since he'd been with her? Her sex clamped down on him as her body pulsated around him. He strained as he felt his own climax approaching, surrounding him, pulling him down with her. He held her to him as if she would slip away if he let go.

He could feel her heart thundering along with his. Her panting echoed in his ear. Slowly, his pulse returned to normal and he eased away from her, holding her to keep her from falling.

When she looked up at him, he smiled. "Hi."

"You definitely know how to greet a girl." Her smile was shy and tentative, even after the weekend they'd shared and what they'd just done on his desk.

"It was probably about time to break in the desk." He brushed his lips across hers as he bent. He pulled up his pants and then picked up her discarded clothing. He held them out to her. Before she could take them, he snatched them out of her reach. "Come back to my place tonight."

A worried look crossed her face. "Do you

think that's smart? What about the paparazzi?"
She reached out for her underwear and shirt.

He held it out of her reach. There had to be
a way. "I'll follow you home, and you can ride
there in my car." He smiled, problem solved.

"Then how do I get home? Can we discuss
this with my underwear on?"

He waggled his eyebrows at her. "I think
some of our best discussions have been when
you aren't wearing underwear."

She laughed. "Usually there's not a lot of
talking at that point."

He waggled his eyebrows again. "I know." He
kissed her soft smile. "Come home with me."

She snatched her clothes from him. "Fine,
but we better not get caught."

"That's part of the fun."

It may be fun, but it definitely wasn't comfortable. Sure the backseat of Chase's car was
plush, but Natalie had been right to worry.
As they pulled up to the gate, she stared out

the tinted back windows at three cars parked along the street with cameras in the windows waiting for the money shot. Butterflies flew haphazardly in her stomach.

Fortunately, no one had followed Chase and her or they would have been caught. Chase had assured her the only reason paparazzi were on his street was the multiple homes that belonged to celebrities.

But Natalie knew at least one reporter who wanted to find out what was going on with Chase. Though they were in the clear tonight, it couldn't possibly last.

She just couldn't imagine not being with Chase every opportunity she had. As they pulled through the gates, her cell phone rang. Rachel.

"Hello?"

"Natalie, are you going to be late tonight?"

She glanced at Chase's eyes in the rearview mirror. "Yeah, I probably won't get in until you're asleep." From the look in Chase's eyes, she probably wouldn't be home until right before Rachel woke up. Her body tightened in anticipation at the promise in his eyes.

"Could you pick up my dry cleaning when you pick up yours tomorrow?"

"Yeah, sure, anything else?"

"Nope that's it. Did you hear that Alexis isn't with your boss anymore? She was seen this weekend, but Chase was nowhere to be found. Do you think he's found someone else?"

Chase pulled into the garage and turned in his seat to look back at her. His eyes sent shivers down her spine.

"I don't know."

"Oh, well, keep me up on the dirt. Talk to you later."

Natalie clicked the End button.

"We did it." Chase opened his door and stepped out. He opened her door. "Not one photo snapped."

She took his offered hand, and he spun her in a circle into his arms. She laughed. She refused to think about tomorrow or next week. This sexy man wanted her now.

But if he wasn't being seen with Alexis… "How long before the press starts to wonder if you're with someone?"

His face turned thoughtful. "They're always speculating. It will probably get intense around the Oscars as they wonder who I'm bringing or who I'm not bringing."

A month until the Oscars. Surely, they'd be out of each other's system in a few weeks.

He led her into the house. A buzzing sound went off in the kitchen. Natalie started and looked around, positive that someone had found them out.

"It's just the gate buzzer." Chase dropped a kiss on her mouth, before moving over to a panel on the wall. He pressed a button. "Hello?"

"Chase, I thought we were going to talk this weekend." Alexis's sultry voice blared through the intercom.

"Alexis, now isn't a good time. Can we talk later?"

Natalie sank into a kitchen chair. Was he trying to juggle two women? Why was she one of them?

"Well, maybe if you'd answered your cell phone when I'd called, I wouldn't have driven all this way."

"Sorry to make you drive, but tonight isn't a good time to talk." Chase sent Natalie an apologetic look.

She smiled tightly. She didn't have the face or body that Alexis had, but Chase didn't seem to care about that. After this weekend and the office… Her face flushed thinking about it. She clasped her hands tightly on the table.

"Oh, I'm sure these nice photographers standing listening to our conversation would love to know why you aren't inviting me up to the house. Wouldn't you, guys?"

Natalie could hear the smile in Alexis's voice.

"Fine, Alexis. Let me buzz you in." Chase released the button and dropped into the chair next to Natalie. His hands covered hers.

"Do you want me to go?" Natalie whispered.

"No, I don't, but I don't want her to see you here."

Her lips tightened, and she tried to ignore the ache in her chest. She started to pull her hands out from under his.

His hands tightened. "Natalie." His voice was soothing. "It's not like that. She would love to cause a scandal where she was the woman wronged, but that's not what this is about. She's trying to get ahead and using me as a stepping stone. She and I were never real. Do you understand that?"

Not looking up, she nodded.

"The only woman I want to be with is you. Why don't you go upstairs and get tucked into bed? I'll be up in a few moments after I get rid of Alexis, and I can show you what we have is real." His finger brushed back a stray hair and then tipped up her chin. "I'll even bring ice cream."

He seemed sincere, but the man acted for a living. She couldn't lie worth a damn, but his career was to pretend and make people believe him. Something in his eyes drew her and reassured her. Maybe she just wanted to be reassured, and he was spewing crap, but she wanted him to be speaking from his heart, even if they were doomed.

"Natalie?"

She focused on his eyes again. Her heart clenched, but she wasn't ready to face the truth. She didn't want him to be using her.

"Please."

She nodded. He brushed his lips over hers. She stood and strode across the kitchen. Without looking back she walked through the dining room and out into the entrance hall where the stairs were.

Even though her eyes were on the marble

tile beneath her feet, she caught a movement out of the corner of her eye. She stopped and looked through the glass door with horror. On the other side stood Alexis, her hand raised to press the doorbell.

They stared at each other through the door. Oh, no.

Chapter Thirteen

Chase had hung back in the kitchen for a few minutes before heading to the door. Alexis had probably stopped and made sure the photographers got a few key shots of her driving through his gate. Maybe even a few on his front porch.

As he entered the foyer, his heart stopped. Natalie and Alexis stared at each other through the glass door. Chase cursed his stupid luck as he brushed past Natalie and jerked open the door.

"Come in, Alexis." He shut the door behind her and led her farther into the room, away from telephoto range, which fortunately Natalie was out of. "Ladies, I believe we need to have a discussion. Let's go to the media room."

Alexis strutted through the door leading to the media room. Chase took Natalie's hand. Her face registered shock and panic.

"I'll fix this."

Her eyes were wide. "How?"

He had no idea how, but he couldn't tell her that. She looked like her dog just died. "I'll fix this."

Taking Natalie's hand, he led her into the Media room and sat her in a chair before closing the door.

"Alexis, I believe you remember Natalie from the office." Chase stood beside Natalie's chair while Alexis leaned against the bar with a satisfied grin.

"From the office? Oh, yes, the little girl who

does the books. Chase, this is worse than Jude's nanny fiasco."

He could see the wheels turning in Alexis's head. "This is nothing like that, Alexis. You and I aren't dating."

"Yes, but you're still screwing the hired help."

Natalie jerked in her chair as if Alexis had slapped her. Why hadn't he asked Natalie to go upstairs and not subject her to Alexis? He rested his hand on her shoulder, and she winced under his hand. He squeezed her, hoping to reassure her. This night was going from bad to worse. "Look, Alexis, we're adults here. You and I aren't a couple anymore."

Alexis's eyes narrowed and her famous lips tightened. "You're right, we're not, but they don't know that." She flung her arm out in an arc. "What *they* will see is that the Sexiest Man Alive prefers his bookkeeper over me. Do you know what that will do to my image?"

"What do you want me to do, Alexis? Put

my life on hold so you can try to make an even bigger name for yourself?"

Her body curled down into a seat. "No, but I think we can find a mutually agreeable solution."

"I'm listening." He didn't need Alexis to start attacking Natalie again, and the quickest way to get Alexis out of here was to figure out what she wanted.

Natalie tensed under his hand again. If he hadn't driven her here, she probably would have already bolted, which would have been impossible to clean up after the entrance Alexis made.

Alexis flashed her smile. "We've already been seen at the Golden Globes."

He waited for her to go on. He'd forgotten how melodramatic she was. Everything had been an act with her. He wondered if she even knew herself anymore.

"There's been Oscar talk...." Her eyes

gleamed with her self-importance. "If you go, I want to be on your arm."

Natalie shifted in the chair. It wasn't a lot to ask. It wasn't as if Natalie wanted to go. Or did she? There's nothing he'd like better than to have her by his side on award night, but that would bring her under the spotlight. She barely wanted to be seen at the best of times. He knew it from the way she'd try to shrink behind things or pull into herself when they spoke.

If their relationship ever hit the stands, it would simultaneously hit a wall. She'd be gone, out of his life forever. He had no doubt about it. His chest ached. It wasn't like this could last.

"Fine. On one condition. My relationship with Natalie stays out of the tabloids. If there is even a hint of her name or face on a page, no Oscar night."

"That's not fair." Alexis stood and stomped her foot to emphasize her point. "What if you guys get sloppy or someone else finds out?"

Chase leaned back against the wall. "That's the risk you'll have to deal with. Take it or leave it." He was confident Alexis would do anything to keep the tabloids from finding out about Natalie just to go to the Oscars. That would at least give Chase a month of not having to worry that Natalie would turn tail and run. One month would have to be enough.

Alexis's mouth curled into a smile. "All right, but you have to go out with me a few times during the month, too." Her red-painted nails curved around her arms like claws.

Make a deal with the devil and you're bound to get burned. Isn't that what his grandpa had always said? If it allowed him to keep Natalie, he'd do almost anything.

"Sure, whatever."

Alexis smiled dangerously. "Seal it with a kiss?"

"Not if my life depended on it." He heard the breath rush out of Natalie. How long had she been holding it?

"Well, then it was a pleasure meeting you again... Natalie, was it? I'll see you this Friday and Saturday, Chase." She drifted across the room.

"Friday only."

She stopped. "Friday night and Saturday dinner. You'll be home early enough to do whatever or whomever you like."

"Fine."

She smiled like the cat that'd caught the canary and swallowed it whole. "It's a pleasure doing business with you, Chase."

Alexis swept from the room. Chase sighed. The arrangement would keep their relationship hidden for a while longer. Natalie could stay.

"Can you take me home?" she whispered. Her voice shook as if she were about to cry.

He dropped to his knee in front of her. Brushing her hair back from her face, he looked up into her large brown eyes. "You don't have to go home, Natalie. Besides, if we leave now, the photogs will definitely follow." Please stay with me, his heart pleaded, even though he knew this couldn't last.

She grimaced.

"Stay, Natalie."

"Why?"

He sensed there was more to that question. Something huge lurked beneath that question, and he wished she'd let it out. Trust him enough to deal with whatever doubts she may be having. He chose to ignore the lurking monster and answer her question as posed, even knowing that lurking monsters usually pounced on you when you least expected it.

"Because I want you to stay. Because I want to hold you tonight. I want to feel you in my arms when I wake."

"Why? Why me?" She refused to meet his eyes. "Why not her?"

He wanted to shake her and pull her into his arms and never let her go. "Because she's not you."

Her face was flush with color. "I'm not like Alexis. I don't want what she wants."

"Natalie, please. We can figure out where this will go tomorrow. Be with me tonight." He wrapped his arms around her waist and laid his head on her chest. "Just tonight."

She wrapped her arms around his head, and he sighed. She was his for at least tonight.

Friday morning came too quickly for Natalie. The week had flown by.

Night Blooming had been nominated for seven Oscars. The whole office was ecstatic. Chase and Robert had taken the production team out to lunch to celebrate the news.

Every night after everyone left, Chase and she had worked on figuring out how much Mr. Morrison had taken. The evidence kept piling up. And after crunching numbers, Chase would take her to his house, and they'd spend the night in each other's arms.

They'd talked about his tutors and her mother.

How their classrooms of one had been lonely at times. He'd shared his secret desire to go to college. She'd told him about rooming with Rachel in college, and how different it had been from anything she'd ever experienced.

She wasn't getting as much sleep as she needed, but she was deliciously tired. During the day, the strutting down the hallway couldn't intimidate her anymore. Her contacts had come in on Monday, and she no longer had to wear her old glasses.

She smiled remembering Chase's reaction. He'd actually missed the darn things and made her promise to bring them with her to his place.

"Are you ready?" Chase was there in front of her.

Her smile grew until she remembered what they were about to do. Martin Morrison was about to get his walking papers. Well, not exactly. There would be a police escort waiting to book him for fraud.

Her smile slipped. She turned her head to look at the door behind her. Chase had insisted she be a part of this, even though she had tried to argue with him. She still wasn't good at saying no.

"Okay." She stood and followed Chase down the hall, trying not to focus on his butt in those fabulous jeans. He stopped abruptly, and she crashed into his back. Steadying herself, she stepped back.

He glanced over his shoulder and smiled the smile that melted her heart every time. She couldn't even blush anymore around him. Except when she thought about what he did to her, his gentle exploration, the slow burn that ignited whenever he was near. She sighed.

"Are we ready?" Robert's voice interrupted her daydreams.

"Yeah, we have all the evidence. We just need to call in Martin. Natalie, you can wait in my office." His voice was all business, but she couldn't seem to lift her gaze from watching his lips move.

His words penetrated her brain, and she nodded and stepped around him into the office. She took one of the chairs along the back and crossed her legs. By the time the men filed in, she'd squeezed her hands so tight her knuckles were turning white.

She didn't want to be in here. Confrontations were not her thing, but Chase had insisted. She tried to fade into the corner as the men took their seats.

"As you know, Martin, we've been looking into the production expenses."

Mr. Morrison glanced over at her in the corner, but didn't so much as raise an eyebrow. He focused his attention on Chase. "Yes, Chase. We finished up the audit on Monday, and I provided you with our report. All the expenses tied in. The numbers were correct."

"Not exactly, Martin." Chase leaned back in

his chair. "We found some things that didn't seem right."

Robert chimed in. "Like expense reports from extras."

"We typically allow actors certain expenses while on set." Martin's voice changed pitch slightly. His head swiveled from Chase to Robert. "I see nothing wrong with a few expenses."

"Martin, we know about the cash payments. We also know that the extras didn't turn in any expense reports." Chase was calm and matter-of-fact. He didn't project the anger or betrayal that Natalie knew he felt. He was cold and direct.

"I don't know what you are suggesting, Chase, but I haven't done anything wrong." He swiveled in his chair and pierced Natalie with his gaze. "What did you find that you didn't bring to me?"

Natalie cowered in her corner. Her palms sweated and her stomach churned.

"Natalie did her job." Chase drew Martin's attention back to him.

She breathed in and out slowly.

Robert stood and walked around the desk behind Chase. "The police are here to take you into custody, Martin. I'm sorry it's come to this."

"Not as sorry as you'll be." Martin stood and straightened his jacket. "Not as sorry as you will be." He glared at Natalie as he walked out the door.

Natalie couldn't slow the beating of her heart and knew it was only a matter of minutes before her breakfast made a repeat performance. She lunged out of the chair and out the door. Shoving into the bathroom, she made it to the stall before the heaving began.

"Natalie?" Chase's voice was directly behind her. His hand soothed her, running down her back.

Mortification filled her as her stomach turned over again. His hand continued slow soothing circles as tears streamed down her face. His hand left her, and a moment later, he draped a wet towel over the back of her neck.

Her stomach finally stopped convulsing. She slid from her knees to lean against the stall wall. Her eyes closed as exhaustion over-whelmed her.

Something wet touched her face, and she jerked her eyes opened. Chase gently wiped her face with a towel. He brushed away a tear with his thumb.

"We need to get you home." His hand smoothed back her hair. He leaned over her as if he were going to pick her up.

She wanted to rely on him, to give in and let him take care of her, but she knew what was on the other side of the bathroom door. Martin's very public exit from the company had drawn a number of press vans. Chase couldn't carry her out of even the bathroom without making a scene. She wasn't prepared to deal with that.

She placed her clammy hand on his warm arm. "No, Chase."

"What?" He seemed genuinely confused.

"You can't. The press."

"Damn it." He slammed his hand against the metal stall. "What does it matter? Maybe I'm just a really good employer."

"That's not the way it works, Chase, and you know it." She pressed her shaking hand against his cheek.

"So now I can't even take care of you." His jaw was tight. He'd push it if she let him.

She wanted to let him and that scared her. Instead she lifted her head. "I'm fine, Chase. It's just nerves. By the way, you know you're in the lady's room, right?"

His eyes narrowed, and he didn't smile like she'd hoped. He stood and helped her to her feet. "Go home, Natalie. Get some sleep."

He tossed the towel in the trash and left the room. She stumbled over to the sink and turned on the faucet. So much for another week or two.

She splashed water over her face and swished some in her mouth to get rid of the taste.

Her makeup was nonexistent. Her face was pale. She had work to do, but the boss had told her to go home. With the hours they'd put in she'd already worked a forty-hour week anyway. She could face the fallout on Monday morning, especially if anyone had witnessed Chase following her into the bathroom.

Besides, Chase was upset with her and she didn't want to face the anger in his eyes.

Did he want to get caught together? She didn't think he did, but she was the one who'd put the restriction on their relationship. He hadn't protested, so she figured he didn't care. She'd thought he understood.

She pushed away from the sink and dried her face. The real problem was for one moment she hadn't cared that the press surrounded the place. She'd just wanted Chase to continue looking at her like that. Concerned and caring.

She'd wanted him to carry her out and take care of her.

Instead she'd go home to her empty apartment. Maybe she'd pop on a movie. She wasn't going to see Chase any other way tonight.

It was Alexis's turn. Her stomach clenched again, but there was nothing left. She definitely had to leave before Alexis came to retrieve her prize.

Chapter Fourteen

Chase's head lolled back on the cab seat. He snapped it upright again. "Here, turn here." He handed the man a hundred-dollar bill as he pulled to the curb. "Keep the change."

His eyes weren't working quite right, but he could still put one foot in front of the other. It had been Alexis's idea to leave his car at her place for the night while they went clubbing. He was really too old to go clubbing. The stairs wavered before him as he climbed them.

He raised his hand and pressed the button.

The chimes rang inside the apartment and he pressed it again. One more time. Why was he pressing this button again? Oh, well, press it again.

"I have a bat and I've called nine-one-one." The sweet sound of Natalie's voice reached his ears.

"Rapunzel, Rapunzel, let down your fair hair."

The door snapped open and the light blinded him. "Chase?"

"Ah, my fair Rosalynn, let me slay a dragon for you, my fair maiden." His grin felt like it would split his face.

He stumbled into the apartment and heard the door shut and the locks snick into place.

"What are you doing here, Chase?" Natalie was suddenly directly in front of him.

"Why, I'm here for you. To slay whatever needs to be slayed. To lay whatever needs to be laid."

Her nose wrinkled, and she raised her

eyebrow. "How did you get here, Chase? Please tell me you didn't drive."

"Of course not. I'm the spokesman for drunk driving. I mean, against drunk driving."

Her image wavered before him, and he reached out to steady her. Maybe those shots hadn't been the smartest move.

"Chase, you can't stay here."

"Why not? A bed is a bed. Your bed is serviceable if I recall. Of course, the floor is good, too. We could always try the wall." He moved in close to her.

Her cheeks turned bright red, and she stepped back right into said wall.

His body flared to life as he noticed her kitten pajamas and a smudge of chocolate on the corner of her mouth. "Do you know I find kitten pajamas very sexy?" He tugged on the hem of her shirt.

"Chase, you should go home. Let me call you a cab." She tried to slide along the wall, but he put his hands on either side of her head. "Chase?"

"What, Natalie? Are you afraid someone will find out? Are you afraid someone will snap a shot of us kissing inside your apartment?" He leaned into her until his mouth brushed against hers when he spoke. "Or are you afraid you'd like being watched?"

"Chase—"

His mouth covered hers, cutting off any protests she might have. He'd had an Altoid in the cab. She tasted like chocolate, smooth and creamy. The mint and chocolate blended perfectly. Her tongue was cold as it brushed against his. Ice cream. He smiled.

He lifted his head. "Did you want me to leave?"

"No." Her voice was light and airy. "But maybe we should go to your place. Rachel will be home soon. And if we leave now maybe the shutterbugs will still be outside the clubs."

Though Chase hadn't always been friendly

with the paparazzi, they were a part of his life. A part he had had to learn to live with and they weren't going away anytime soon. It didn't matter tonight. All he wanted was Natalie.

He brushed back a strand of brown hair and tucked it behind her ear. "Why don't you drive us back?"

Her eyes fluttered as she leaned into his hand. She turned her head and kissed his open palm.

"How soon did you say your roommate would be home?" He rubbed his thumb across her lips.

"Too soon."

He replaced his thumb with his lips. She opened beneath him. Her hands gripped his shirt and pulled him closer. He gathered her into his arms and backed her down the hallway.

He dragged in a breath. "Haven't we been here before?" he said as he pushed through the living room door.

Her smile took his breath away. "I'm sure I have no idea what you mean."

As he traced the sensual curve of her lower lip with his fingertip, he glanced over her shoulder and saw the credits rolling on *If Only.* "At least this time you got to finish."

Her eyes sparkled up at him. "I always finish with you." Wherever this playful woman had come from, he hoped she'd stick around for a while. His beautiful accountant seemed to be blooming all around him.

She took his hand and pulled him toward her bedroom. He went willingly. Even though he'd had a few shots, the effects were starting to fade, leaving behind that easy, relaxed feeling.

He sank on the edge of the bed and held his arms out to her. She stepped between his knees, and he wrapped his arms around her.

"I'm sorry," she whispered as her hands stroked over his hair. Her heartbeat was strong beneath the cushion of her breasts.

"For what?" He never wanted to let her go, but knew it was coming. The pressure of a public relationship would kill this tender thing they had. His arms squeezed her tighter.

"For being so damned paranoid." Her hand brushed the side of his face.

He closed his eyes and absorbed what she was making him feel. His heart filled his chest and he knew he wouldn't be able to let her go. He lifted his head and took her face between his hands. "All I want is you, Natalie."

Their lips met. He surrendered himself to whatever would happen in the future as he pulled her down to the bed with him.

"What was that?" Natalie put her hand against Chase's glistening shoulder. "Chase?"

His head lifted from her breasts, and he looked at her with passion-laden eyes. His body brushed against hers, tantalizing all the fine nerve endings as he moved up to take possession of her mouth again. The sound receded in her mind as he slid into her, filling her.

The sound of the door slamming shocked Natalie. "Chase?"

He moved within her. "Hmmm." His movements were slow and lazy. She got lost in the movements as her passion swirled higher and higher with each stroke.

"Natalie, why are all the lights on?" Rachel's voice pierced through the wood of her door.

"Uh-oh."

Rachel knew no boundaries. She could open the door and find them. Chase's naked body completely covered hers. Not that Rachel hadn't seen Chase's butt before. Almost every woman in America and across the globe had seen Chase's butt. Her body tensed at the combined approach of her orgasm and the footsteps outside the door.

"Chase?" she whispered. She groaned against his lips. He seemed determined to drive her out of her mind, and he was doing a great job of it, too. His lips moved over hers, capturing whatever she might have said. Her body exploded all around him.

He swallowed all the sounds she made. His body tensed over her, and he let go.

"Are you even here, Natalie?" Rachel's voice was on the other side of the door.

Natalie started pushing on Chase. He had to get off her before Rachel opened the door. He cuddled against her body and a little snore escaped his mouth.

"I'm not dressed, Rachel." That much was true. "Sorry, I…" *I just had incredible sex with Chase Booker and can't tell anyone.* "I spilled ice cream all over myself."

The arms around her tightened. Chase rolled until she was on top of his chest. Oh, yeah, this was a much better view for Rachel. She lifted her head to glare down at him and found his laughing green eyes open.

The urge to shove him off the bed almost

overwhelmed her. She tried to scoot off his chest, but his arms held her still.

She turned her head to watch the doorknob. Her ear was next to his mouth and she about jumped when his quiet voice whispered, "I'd lick the ice cream off for you."

"Oh, okay." Rachel's voice drifted away from the door. She must be walking away. "I'm going to head to bed. We have to talk in the morning. I can't wait to tell you what I found out about Chase."

"I bet you could tell her a thing or two." He sucked her earlobe into his mouth, sending shivers of pleasure rippling through her.

The door to the other bedroom closed, and Natalie relaxed against Chase's chest. Sure, she could tell Rachel that Chase was an unselfish lover. He snored. He was ticklish on his sides. His lips were as soft as velvet. He slept wrapped around her as if he never wanted to let her go. And she was hopelessly in love with him.

She rested her head against the steady beat of his heart. One of his hands stroked down her back while the other rested in her hair. She'd been wrong. She should have stopped earlier. She should have never gone to his house. She should have turned him away at her door. She should have stopped that first kiss.

She was too far gone now. When she thought of ending it, her lungs seized up, and she fought for air. She shivered as she thought of the long, lonely nights ahead of her. Lonely nights made worse because she knew what it was like to not be alone. To be made love to so thoroughly that no one would ever be able to replace him.

Her eyes burned, and she took short, quick breaths to stop the flood that threatened. He rolled them to the side and lifted her chin. Seeing the concern in his eyes broke her. The tears slipped out even as she fought to hold them back.

"What's wrong, Natalie?" His thumb

brushed aside the tears, smearing them on her cheeks.

"Nothing." *Everything.* She tried to smile and blinked back the tears. Maybe it was worth the risk. Maybe he was worth the exposure. And maybe she could have a pony, too.

He tightened his arms around her, pulling her against his chest. "Let's go home," he whispered against her hair.

Not his house. Home. The place she belonged.

Chapter Fifteen

Natalie sipped the hot tea Chase had made her. Wearing only his T-shirt, she sat on his kitchen counter while he cooked eggs for her on his industrial range.

The world seemed bright and cheery this morning like nothing could touch them. He worked on the stove like a pro, cooking an omelet without a spatula, showing off by sliding it around the pan before flipping it in the air and catching it.

"You wouldn't do that if you had to clean

up the mess." She set the mug down and used her hands to brace herself while she leaned back.

He glanced up at her. "I don't make messes that I don't clean up." His free hand roamed tantalizingly up her thigh toward the hem of the T-shirt.

She playfully swatted at his hand. "None of that. I need some food before another round."

"Thankfully, food is done." He eased the omelet onto a plate and turned off the stove. He grabbed her waist and lifted her down to the floor.

"My hero." She grabbed her plate and went to the kitchen table.

Chase joined her with a wicked smile on his face. "Eat up."

The man might be an Academy Award-winning actor, but he could cook one mean omelet. Of course, it helped that he had all the finest ingredients and fresh vegetables to pick from.

The shrill ring of the phone broke the amicable silence. Chase got up and left the room to pick it up.

A few seconds later "Glamorous" by Fergie sounded from the depths of her purse. Setting down her fork, she dug out her phone. A picture of Rachel showed on the screen.

She hit the Talk button. "You changed my ringtone."

"Not now. Where are you?" Rachel's voice was impatient.

Natalie leaned against the wall and looked down the hall to where Chase stood talking on the phone. She could feel the silly smile on her face and didn't care. "Having breakfast."

"Where?"

"Why?"

"Natalie, do you know what's going on?" Rachel seemed upset by something.

"No, what's happened? Are you okay?" She straightened from the wall. Chase's eyes widened as his gaze met hers.

"That CFO Chase fired talked to some reporter and said that Chase was having an affair with someone at work."

Natalie's heart stopped. She almost dropped the phone. "Do they know who?" Her voice sounded distant to her own ears.

"They say whoever it is he's been seeing her and Alexis. Do you want to tell me something, Natalie?" Rachel was her best friend. Natalie could hear the hurt in Rachel's voice.

"Where do they say Chase is?"

Chase had set down the phone and was striding across the room toward her.

"They think he's at Alexis's. At least, that's what one report says. But another report says an eyewitness saw him get into a cab and leave Alexis. They haven't been able to talk to the cabby yet."

Natalie broke out in a cold sweat. Thousands of cameras could be lined up all over the street just waiting for her to step out of his house. The delicious omelet sat like a lump in her stomach. Chase stopped in front of her.

"I've got to go." She shut the phone on Rachel's voice.

"They know," she said. The illusion shattered around her. It was over. "I've got to go."

Chase grabbed her shoulders before she could walk around him. "Why?"

What did he mean why? Didn't he know? "They know, Chase. Martin leaked it to the press. They are probably out on the street, just waiting for me to walk out. Oh, God, they are going to take pictures of me."

"Natalie?" His fingers tightened on her shoulders.

"What, Chase?" She glanced at the windows. Photographers might be lurking in the bushes, behind the trees. "Maybe they aren't here yet. Maybe I can still get out."

"I talked to Alexis."

Her gaze shot to his. The look in his eyes

didn't alleviate her panic. This was worse than she thought.

"She's leaked to the paparazzi that I spent the night at her house. They're waiting over there to talk to me. She's putting them off, but she has to go out sometime today."

Relief flowed over her in a gush. "Then I can leave. I can get out before they realize you are here. No one's going to think anything of my little Honda leaving. They'll just think I'm the paid help."

"You aren't the hired help." His voice was forceful. "Don't go."

"I can get dressed—what?" She refocused on him.

His face was drawn tight as if he was fighting with something. "Don't go."

"But if I don't, they'll find out." Where was he going with this?

"So what? Let them find out." A hardness filled his eyes.

She stared up at him. Her mouth parted to ask why, but no sound came out.

He closed his eyes and dropped his hands from her shoulders. "You're right. Go get dressed. I'll clean up down here."

He turned his back on her and walked to the kitchen table. She didn't want this to end, but the situation had spiraled out of her control. She wanted to go to him and wrap her arms around his waist and say everything would be okay, but he'd already closed himself off from her.

She drew in a breath. She had to go. There was nothing more to it. Their affair had been fun to Chase while it was hidden, but he'd realize she wasn't what he wanted in the bright glare of the spotlight. The carefree days were over. She had to let Chase go.

Chase slammed the refrigerator door. He wanted to throw plates across the room. He wanted to tear something apart. Instead he leaned his forehead against the stainless steel door.

She was leaving. Damn it. He couldn't stop her. She never wanted to be part of his world. His shrinking violet preferred the dark to the glare of the spotlight.

He'd known that from the start. They'd both known this would happen. This time would have come eventually; he'd just thought when it happened she'd want to stay, or he'd be ready to let her go.

He shoved away from the fridge and stormed through the house. He took the stairs two at a time until he reached the bedroom.

She sat on the bed looking forlorn. "I found my sock." She held it up. "But I can't find my other shoe." Her lower lip trembled.

Scanning the room, his gaze fell upon the missing shoe. He scooped it up and knelt on the floor at her feet. She wouldn't meet his eyes.

He snatched the sock out of her loose fingers.

Lifting her foot, he pulled her sock over it and then slipped on her shoe. He stood, tugging her up with him.

She studied his chest. He tipped her face up so he could look into her brown eyes one last time. Tears swam over her eyes.

One more taste. His lips found hers. Her arms wrapped around his neck, holding him close. Desperation tainted the kiss.

She yanked her head away and dropped her arms. "Good-bye, Chase." She hurried out the door.

A pain stabbed through his chest. What if…

He caught up to her at the bottom of the stairs. "Wait."

She stopped and dropped her chin to her chest. "Don't make this any harder than it already is."

"How much harder can it get?" He could hear the tremor in his voice, but ignored it. All that mattered was that Natalie didn't give up on him.

"Please, Chase. Let me go." She moved in the direction of the kitchen, but he blocked her. She swung around toward the front door.

He grabbed her arm. "I love you." The words slipped from his soul.

She stiffened as if he'd hit her, but she didn't meet his eyes. The words lay like a gauntlet thrown down between them. He hadn't meant to say them. He wasn't even sure what those words meant, but it felt right with Natalie.

Her words were whispered to the door. "You pretend to be in love for a living." Her arm shook under his touch. "How do you know what's real?"

Her words cut him to the quick. He drew her away from the door and turned her. He tilted her face up. Tears streamed down from huge eyes. Her eyes were devoid of hope. It ripped through him.

"You're real. What I feel is real." How

could he convince her? What more could he give her?

She closed her eyes and shook her head. "Pretend. Make believe." She jerked her arm from him and swiped at her cheeks. "Someone to play house with. Someone to pretend to have a normal life. You'll never have a normal life. You're Chase Booker, movie star, producer—"

"I'm a man, dammit." Chase could feel the years slip away, and he was that teenage boy trying to explain to his girlfriend to ignore the cameras. They didn't matter. Only the two of them did.

Natalie tried to walk past him to go to the garage again, but he blocked her way. He pulled her into his arms and kissed her. She jerked away with tears in her eyes, pressing her fingers to her lips.

"We can't, Chase. We can't be in love. We don't live in the same world." She spun and yanked open the front door.

"Fine." He wouldn't crucify himself any-more. If she wanted to leave, she'd leave. If his love wasn't enough to keep her, she could go.

Her shoulders slumped and she nodded. She glanced back over her shoulder at him, but he maintained a look of indifference. He'd begged enough.

As she looked forward again, a flash went off.

Chapter Sixteen

"Back to our catch of the day," the television blared. "It would appear Alexis Brandt has been replaced by a younger woman. Photographers got these pictures of the young woman leaving Chase's house earlier today. The woman hasn't been identified yet. Friday, allegations of an office romance had been released by Pandora Productions' ex-CFO, Martin Morrison."

The TV showed Natalie's Honda Fit racing out of Chase's driveway. What it didn't show was that she'd managed to get away before anyone was able to hop into their cars. She'd driven around a little before returning home, just in case.

Why had she gone out the front door? Because she couldn't stand to walk around Chase and through his house to escape. Because if she'd walked through his house, he might have changed her mind, and she would have stayed.

"We don't have to watch." Rachel plopped down on the couch next to her and handed her a bucket of Cherry Garcia ice cream and a spoon. Rachel swiped at the used tissues that littered the couch and the floor.

"I know." Her insides were hollow. It didn't matter. None of it mattered. Chase had told her he loved her, and she'd thrown it back in his face. Because she thought it was for the best.

"Do you want to talk about it?" Rachel straightened the blanket over Natalie's legs.

"No." The tears overflowed her eyes again. It hadn't been for the best, because the paparazzi were going to figure out who she was. She couldn't avoid work. She'd promised Chase she would carry the workload until they could hire a CFO.

"Wanna watch a movie?"

"No." Her favorite movie that saw her through the bad times would never be the same again. She couldn't watch Chase on the screen and not remember those same eyes staring into hers, that body pressed against hers, those words.… Those simple words that meant everything to her, but weren't enough.

Natalie and Rachel decided if she wore her glasses maybe the swarms of paparazzi wouldn't be able to recognize her. She'd pulled her hair back in a ponytail. It had been down when she'd left Saturday morning and had obscured part of her face.

Natalie could barely breathe let alone walk and talk. A sense of numbness surrounded her. She borrowed Rachel's car to get to work.

When she pulled up to Pandora Productions, it was worse than she'd imagined. A crew from *E!* stood outside recording an intro piece. The parking lot was filled with photographers leaning against their cars waiting.

She hoped they wouldn't realize she was the woman they were waiting for. She parked the car and steadied herself. Pushing her glasses up her nose, she walked toward the door.

"Chase Booker and Robert Addler brought allegations of fraud against their CFO on Friday morning."

She breezed past the camera crew and made it through the door. The receptionist glanced up at her and went back to the computer screen.

Shrugging her purse back over her shoulder, Natalie shuffled down the hallway to her desk. She flipped on the computer and glanced around. No one felt the urge to strut this morning, which suited Natalie just fine. She didn't need to be reminded she wasn't tall, thin and gorgeous on top of everything else.

Her water bottle was empty, but there was no way she was going to pass by Chase's office to get more water. What if he was in there? She had to pretend he didn't matter.

She opened her e-mail, and the computer downloaded two messages. Both were from Jared Anderson. Sighing, she clicked on the first one. It was his contact information, along with a note of how they'd talked on the phone.

She closed it and opened the second one, which had been sent this morning. *If you need to talk, you know where to find me. S*he deleted the e-mail. It was inevitable that people would put two and two together and figure out she was the one Chase had been seeing.

But she wasn't going to help them along. She pulled a stack of invoices over and started to enter them into the computer. She needed to keep herself busy.

Walking into Pandora had been a nightmare of saying "No comment" and "I have nothing to say." His sunglasses helped to hide the rings under his eyes from his sleepless night.

He'd already told his publicity director to give no comments. Alexis had agreed to keep Natalie's name a secret as long as she could say that she dumped him and the office worker was a rebound. He hadn't cared. Business as usual.

The receptionist glanced up and gave him a wan smile before returning to her work. He walked up to her and waited for her to hang up the phone.

"Hold all my calls. If anyone asks, Robert and I will have a press release this afternoon about Martin's departure." He'd been so wrapped up in Natalie that he hadn't even thought about firing Martin, which had served to increase the number of reporters outside.

"Yes, sir." She dropped her eyes back to the computer screen and answered the line.

He straightened his shoulders. Natalie would be here already. He had to keep her secret for as long as possible. The hallway was mostly empty as he walked toward his office.

He glanced nonchalantly toward Natalie's desk. Her head was bent over some papers and her glasses dangled on the tip of her nose. He almost stumbled, but ripped his gaze from her and continued forward.

Taking a deep breath, he unlocked his office. Ten minutes after he settled behind his desk to read a script, Robert came in.

"We need to talk."

Chase set down the script. He hadn't been able to read it anyway. The image of Natalie half-naked on his desk kept interrupting his train of thought. "What's on your mind?"

"Are the rumors true?" Robert slumped into the chair.

"Which ones?" Chase looked up at the ceiling. He should have stayed home, but every room smelled of her. Her smile followed him. Her words haunted his steps.

"Well, let's see. How about the ones that

include a certain accountant?" Robert had been his friend for years. Part of the reason they became friends was his no-nonsense attitude.

But Chase didn't want to talk about Natalie. He tightened his lips and leaned back.

Robert shifted. "Okay, how about damage control? You know, the other employees are talking about how she slept with you to get the CFO position."

"That's ridiculous."

Robert held out his hands. "I'm only saying what they're saying. You need to figure out how to handle this and quick. There are leaks in this company that would make a sieve jealous. The press is going to find out about Natalie, and it's going to blow up in both of your faces unless you do something about it now."

Chase dropped his head into his hands. "I know, but what am I supposed to do?"

"Don't tell me you love her? I thought you were just getting over Alexis." Robert held up his hands again.

Chase stopped glaring at Robert, but he still wasn't happy. It would be a while before he was happy again. "We'll deal with it when we deal with Martin."

"We should also consider changing who she reports to."

Chase slammed his hand down on the desk.

Robert stood up. "She'll start reporting to me. We'll start interviewing for the CFO position tomorrow. I already told Anne to call recruiters."

"We're not together anymore. She can still report to me." Chase rubbed his hands over his face, feeling his hard-earned control slipping.

"It doesn't matter if you are still together or not. We have to maintain appearances. And maybe if she isn't reporting to you, she might actually stay with the company. If you hadn't noticed, she has a good mind and a knack for numbers."

"I noticed."

"Good, then we'll move forward with my plan." Robert moved to the door and looked back. "Man, you must have it bad." He slipped out. Chase's pen hit the closed door.

The whole morning he stayed in his office trying to get through the script. Every few minutes someone else would knock on his door. By noon he was a mess of tension.

He'd finally managed to put aside the disaster his life had become and get into the script when a tentative knock on the door brought him out of it.

"What?" Chase bellowed at the door.

The door opened a crack. "Um, if now isn't a good time, I could come back later." Natalie stood in the doorway, looking like she'd prefer to run down the hall than come in and talk with him.

"Why are you here?" he snapped. Chase's heart beat unsteadily in his chest. The smell of strawberries wafted between them, making him want to grind his teeth together.

A tinge of pink covered her cheeks and neck. She slid her glasses back up her nose. "Robert asked me to meet him here." She glanced toward Robert's office. Her uncertainty and discomfort made him feel a little better, but it also annoyed him.

He'd covered her blushes with his kisses. Brought smiles and sighs to those lips. Slipped his hands around her waist and held her body against him.

"Maybe I should wait in the hallway...." Her voice brought his attention back to her face.

"Don't be ridiculous. Have a seat. I'm sure Robert will be here in a minute."

Natalie considered turning tail and running for the door. Chase's intense gaze turned her knees to water, while it caused her battered heart to leap up in her throat. She glanced once more toward Robert's office and then at her watch. He'd said noon. It was five past.

She couldn't make any more excuses. Her

legs were stiff as she walked into Chase's office and perched on the edge of the chair. Her cheeks were on fire, even more so when his gaze dipped down to her breasts. Having not gotten the memo, her body responded instantly.

She pressed her knees together and straightened her skirt. Her hands turned white from clutching them together, and her stomach started to churn, just like the last time she'd been in here.

"Relax, Natalie. I'm not going to pounce on you."

Her gaze jerked to his eyes. She remembered him saying that to her before. She couldn't place when, but it raised the ghost of Saturday morning. The things she'd said. Her gaze dropped to her lap.

The urge to run out the door raced through her, but she stayed. Chase didn't say anything else, but she could feel his eyes on her. The silence relentlessly continued. Maybe she could come back later? Or he could call her when Robert came in. She raised her head to suggest it, but stopped before saying anything.

Pain. For a moment, his eyes seemed like an open wound. A wound she'd caused. But then it was gone like she'd imagined it. Maybe she had. He couldn't possibly love her. It just didn't make sense. As soon as the next actress crossed his path, he'd be fine. He probably wouldn't even remember her name. A pain stabbed through her heart at the thought.

"Sorry, I got caught up on a phone call." Robert swept into the office and closed the door. "Wow, you could cut the tension with a knife in here."

Chase broke their eye contact to glare at Robert. "What is this about, Robert?"

Robert smiled. "Well, I figured if we were going to ruin this woman's life she should be prepared."

"What?" Natalie's hand began to shake.

Robert gave her a sympathetic smile and

reached over as if to take one of her hands. A growl from the other side of the desk stopped him.

"We have to make this go away, and the only way to make something go away in Hollywood is to be up-front and honest so there is nothing to find. Then wait for some huge, new scandal for them to sink their teeth into."

Natalie's heart tightened, and her gaze flitted to Chase's stern face. His lips were pressed into a thin line.

"Natalie," Robert began, "we have to put all the facts out there. Chase has already said your relationship is over, which will make the press only wonder why it ever happened and probably make them back off. Especially if they think it was just another boss-banging-the-worker story."

Natalie winced at the harsh words. Chase had told Robert they were over? She'd known when she left Saturday there'd be no turning back, but it didn't stop the shooting pain through her heart or the upheaval in her stomach.

"You'll be reporting to me from now on and the new CFO when hired. I suggest that both of you—" Robert's fatherly stare went between them "—stay away from each other. The less you are seen together the more seriously our statement today will be taken."

"That won't be a problem. I'm going to help Reggie in Ontario later this week. He's been having issues with some of the scenes." Chase brushed his hand through his hair.

Her fingers itched to smooth it back down. Something she'd never do again. He was leaving? For how long?

"That's a good idea. With you gone, the focus should go with you. What about the luncheon next week? Our nominations?"

Chase stood and walked to look out the window. "I'll be back for it."

Natalie could feel the tears rising, and her

stomach rolled, as well. She cleared her throat. "If that's...if that's all, I'll go to lunch."

Robert gave her a sympathetic look and nodded. "Sure, Natalie. Why don't you go home for the rest of the day? I think after the news conference this afternoon things are going to get crazy here."

"Thank you." She rose and walked to the door. She glanced back at Chase's profile. "Have a good trip."

"Are you sure?" Rachel eyed her as if she'd gone out of her mind.

Maybe she had. Maybe she'd lost it the moment she'd run into Chase that first day. If not her mind, she'd definitely lost her heart.

Natalie set her pizza down on her plate. More comfort food that just wasn't comforting. She shoved the plate across the coffee table and pulled her blanket tighter around her shoulders.

"I've got to know what they are saying. I

need to be prepared for tomorrow." Natalie's eyes were dry, too dry. The kind of dryness that only happened after all the tears were gone.

Still watching her, Rachel clicked the remote for the TV and turned her laptop on. The bright light from the TV hurt Natalie's eyes, but she didn't care. Chase had caught a flight out in the afternoon, that much she knew.

"In a surprising turn of events, Pandora Productions in the news again shortly after their nomination for Best Picture for their production *Night Blooming*. The company has brought charges of fraud against their former CFO, Martin Morrison."

A picture of Mr. Morrison being escorted from the building appeared on the screen behind Ryan Seacrest.

"Shortly after his arrest, Morrison leaked to the press that Chase Booker, co-owner of Pandora, had been having an affair with one of his staff."

A shot of her escape from Chase's house Saturday came up on the screen. She curled tighter into the corner of the couch. Clips of Alexis and Chase started to show on the screen.

"Alexis Brandt stated today that she and Chase never really got back together, and she was as shocked as everyone else by this turn of events. This afternoon, Chase Booker and Robert Addler spoke with *E!*"

The screen cut to the news conference. Chase stood behind Robert as he spoke to the crowd. "We have turned all our evidence on Martin Morrison over to our lawyer and the police. We were sad to see Martin go as we had always considered him an asset before all this came to light."

Robert glanced back at Chase before returning to the microphones. "We are currently looking for a replacement CFO. We will not be promoting anyone within the company. In addition, we have shifted the accounting department to be more fully under my direction. This will enable Chase to spend more time in the field and to star in more films."

He shifted behind the podium. "Martin also claimed an ongoing affair between Chase and one of our staff. Chase was trying to protect the woman from the misguided attention of the paparazzi. Regardless, the affair is over, and the woman would prefer to remain anonymous. I would hope that the press would respect her and Chase's privacy in this matter. Thank you."

The TV cut back to the studio. "We were also told that Chase would be going to Ontario to help work on Pandora Productions' filming. Meanwhile, Britney Spears—"

Rachel hit Mute on the remote. "Okay, here's what the entertainment news is saying. Some say you were a rebound and the real reason he's going to Ontario is to see Madeline Stark, who recently dumped Andre Pratt."

"Do you think that's why he went?" The tears

began to burn at the back of her throat again. Had she really just been a rebound?

"I don't know, sweetie." Rachel rubbed her hand on Natalie's leg in a comforting way.

Natalie fought down the tears. "What are they saying about me?"

"Let's see." Rachel's eyes roamed the page as her hand moved the mouse. "Here's something. They suspect you are the woman in the picture, but no one will confirm it. A source, one of your stupid coworkers, claims that you and Chase worked late for the past two weeks and seemed very chummy in the office."

Natalie picked at the threads coming out at the end of the blanket. She needed to know more. She needed to know why Chase had picked her. She needed to know why he'd been with her. "What else does it say?" she choked out around the held-back tears.

"Natalie, I don't think you want to know." Rachel shut the lid on the laptop. "It's just the normal catty stuff."

"The stuff you enjoy?"

Rachel brushed a stray piece of Natalie's hair behind her ear. "Only when it's about someone ridiculous, which you aren't. Are you sure you don't want to talk about it? I swear I won't leak it to the press." She smiled softly.

"I know you won't." Natalie tried to return her friend's smile but wasn't sure if it came across. "I just…I want to understand, is all."

"Understand what?"

"Why me?" A tear slipped over the edge. The rest of the tears, seeing the escapee, pressed forward.

Rachel handed her a tissue. "Why not you, Natalie? You're bright, intelligent, loving, pretty. You take care of anyone you care about. What's not to love about you, Natalie?"

The tissues kept coming as Natalie's vision blurred behind the tears. "He said he loved me." She sniffled. "He said he loved me, and I said he didn't."

Chapter Seventeen

The week that followed was the hardest of Natalie's life. From the guy digging around in her trash to the car that followed her to work, at first she wondered if she was just paranoid. When a camera flashed as she left the grocery store, she knew she wasn't.

It was so subtle she barely noticed it at first. Rachel kept showing Natalie pictures of her when she hadn't even known anyone was around. The receptionist held all calls to Natalie's phone.

Robert had been especially nice to her and had even had a meeting with the staff informing them that the new CFO would start in two weeks. Natalie buried herself in the piles of paper. Eventually the strutting down the hall picked up again, and people didn't stop talking when she came into the room.

Her heart ached every time she passed Chase's empty office. It had to be easier than actually seeing him every day. Rachel stopped informing Natalie of Chase's comings and goings when she continued to break down into tears and run from the room.

Natalie sighed with relief as the hour turned to four. One more hour and then she'd have the whole weekend to lock herself away with tubs of ice cream and her favorite mov—

Pushing aside the folder on her desk, she realized she couldn't watch her favorite movie. The constant ache in her chest throbbed. Maybe she'd rent some horror flicks instead, or a good chick flick.

Her phone rang, and she didn't think twice about picking it up. "This is Natalie."

"Natalie, Jared Anderson. Before you hang up, give me a minute of your time."

She held the phone to her ear instead of slamming it down. "I'm listening."

"Good. Why don't we meet somewhere? You could get your side of the relationship on record. It could launch your career. At least get you on a reality show."

Her mind blanked. "Is that all you people think about? Do you really think I like having my name in headlines or my face in your papers? Well, I don't. I don't want to be any part of this industry. I'm an accountant, for Pete's sake. Not someone waiting for her big break. I'll thank you to never call me again."

She slammed the phone down and felt better than she had all week.

"Nice job." The voice stilled her heart.

She couldn't look up. She wasn't ready. She couldn't see him. She couldn't resist. Her gaze trailed up the jean-clad hips to his black T-shirt, the planes of his body as familiar as her own.

Her heart pounded within her chest. His lips were curved into a wary smile and his eyes… Why did they have to be so green? "Chase." His name slipped out of her mouth on a sigh.

"I heard what you said."

Had she been talking? His eyes appeared tired, and there was a strain around his lips.

"Sorry?" Her brain had flown out the window when she'd heard his voice again.

"The reporter? I couldn't have said it better myself." He pointed toward the phone and her gaze followed, completely dumbfounded.

Heat rushed into her cheeks as his words sunk in. "Oh."

"I've got to…" He gestured down the hall with his thumb.

"I hope you had a good trip."

He nodded and disappeared down the hall. She dropped her head down to the desk. So much for being intelligent. What was he doing back? What had he been doing? Did he hook up with that actress up there?

She lifted her head and grabbed her cell phone. If any one person knew all the goings-on in Hollywood, it would be Rachel.

Chase closed the door behind him and leaned his forehead against it. It had to be the best performance of his life. Pretending he wasn't falling apart without Natalie. If he could convince her, he could convince everyone else.

Her eyes had been wide and tired. Good. He hoped she wasn't getting any sleep, because he wasn't. When he would finally drift off, he'd reach out to pull her close, and she wasn't there.

He dropped his briefcase inside the door and collapsed into his chair. His head in his hands, he ignored the knocking on his door.

The door opened. "Why did you come in at all?"

"Leave me alone, Robert."

The door shut. "The director called to say you left earlier than expected." Robert was trying to lead Chase, but Chase didn't feel like discussing the real reason he'd left early. He'd been drawn back like a moth to a flame.

He wanted to see her before the weekend. When he'd walked in and seen her behind the mountain of paper, his heart had lifted. Then he'd heard her on the phone with the reporter, and he remembered.

She didn't want to be in the public eye. She had no intention of ever being in the public eye. There was no future for them. But he'd managed to stand there and act as if his chest weren't ready to explode.

"So you aren't going to say anything?" Robert sank into the chair. "Are you going to ask about the new CFO?"

Chase leaned back in his chair and narrowed his eyes on Robert. "You sent me the résumé. We did the interview via conference call. Is there something I missed? You called every day."

"No, Chase, you called every day. You avoided talking about Natalie every time, as well. You look like hell, man."

"I just got off a plane—"

"And you rushed over here to—what? Sit in your office and rest your weary head? Give me a break. I saw you stop at Natalie's desk—"

"I just was checking up—"

"You stood there like a man presented with water after crossing the desert. Why not talk to her? Her eyes are red and puffy every morning. You both are hurting, so why not end the games and just get together already."

Chase stared at his partner with astonishment. "She doesn't want any part of the fame or this industry."

"We're not talking about the industry. We're talking about you, Chase."

"The industry and me are the same. It's always been a part of who I am. A part I can't escape, and I don't want to escape it. I may hate being followed sometimes, but it's part of my life and she doesn't want any of that."

"Have you asked her?"

Chase could feel the rage rising within him. "Why would she? That part of my life is never going away. Even if I had never gone into acting, I would still be the son of Matt Booker and Madeline Caine. If she doesn't want that life, we can't be together."

Natalie was having difficulty breathing. When someone moved down the hall, she'd hold her breath and not release it until she knew it wasn't Chase. This had to be the longest hour of her life.

Since it was Friday a lot of the staff took off early. People were constantly going past her desk. Rachel had at least eased her fears that Chase hadn't already moved on. Not that she cared, but it had made her feel better to know he hadn't dived right back into the dating pool.

Of course, that could also mean that he really did love her, which made her feel even worse.

Life shouldn't be so hard. He'd gone out of his way to keep their relationship discreet, which was what she wanted. Wasn't it? Someone started down the hall.

Hold it, hold it. Just another model. Release. This was ridiculous. She glanced at the clock. Close enough. She bent and got her purse, and when she came back up she screamed. Not a bloodcurdling scream, but that oh-my-God-you-scared-the-last-year-off-my-life scream. Chase stood in front of her desk.

Her hand covered her racing heart, and she took several deep breaths.

"I didn't mean to startle you." His smooth voice awakened the desire that was always on simmer just for him.

Her face flushed as hot flashes of him making love to her burst within her mind. "Not a problem," she said hurriedly. She clutched her purse to her like a shield as she stood up. "I was just leaving." Did he know she was picturing him naked?

"Natalie."

She stopped and stared at the ground. Please don't come near. She could survive hearing his voice, but she'd explode into tears if he touched her. Or worse, she'd throw herself into his arms and plead with him to forgive her.

Her eyes squeezed shut when she felt him move behind her. She wasn't this strong. She could bolt. She could run for the door and pray she didn't trip.

"Can I…"

Can he what? She lifted her face and stared straight ahead at the door. "I really should be going."

"Can I walk you to your car?"

She spun and almost fell back. She hadn't realized he was directly behind her. He reached out to steady her by her elbow, but she jerked out of his reach and banged her elbow against the wall.

"Are you okay?" He reached out to steady her.

She pressed herself against the wall avoiding his hands and held her elbow as her funny bone throbbed. "I'm fine."

"From that face you're making, I highly doubt that." He dropped his hands.

Her body relaxed. His eyes were resigned when she finally lifted her gaze to meet them.

"We can't be friends, can we?" His shoulders dropped.

"I…" She wanted to tell him they could. She didn't want to let him out of her life, but she couldn't be with him and not watch his lips and remember. She shook her head and said softly, "I don't think so."

He nodded. "Can I walk you out?"

The door was a long way away, but outside a few stubborn photographers lingered, waiting for just the right photo op. "I don't think so, Chase."

His smile was a shadow of the one he used to give her. "You are probably right. Have a good weekend." His hand lifted as if to brush her cheek.

Her breath caught, and she couldn't move. He dropped his hand and spun on his heel, leaving her in the hall with a throbbing elbow and a broken heart.

"I know you're in there." Rachel yelled through the door.

"No, I'm not," Natalie told her pillow. She hugged the pillow closer, knocking a dozen tissues off the edge of the bed. It still smelled like him. It was only a throw pillow, but it smelled like him.

"I don't have to go out of town. I can tell the company I have personal business to attend to." Her voice was muffled by the door.

"You need to go. I'll be fine."

"I got more ice cream." There wasn't enough chocolate ice cream in the world to make the pain go away, but Rachel didn't need to know that. "I'll have my cell phone on. If you need me, call. I don't care when or why. I'll answer. I also picked up some of those frozen meals that are low-fat. You know, to counteract the ice cream."

"Thank you." She lifted her face from the pillow. "Go. I'll be fine."

"Okay, I'll see you Wednesday. Try to get out of bed sometime between now and then."

Natalie waited until the door closed and she heard the snick of the locks. She pried herself off the bed and wandered into the living room. Grabbing the remote, she cued up *If Only* and wandered into the kitchen to grab a fresh carton of ice cream.

There was a note on the fridge. *Try to eat something besides ice cream. R.* "Well, chocolate sauce isn't ice cream."

She piled her blanket, the pillow that smelled like Chase and her ice cream onto the couch with her as the beginning credits rolled.

She found herself caught up by the story. The pressure on her chest lifted as the love affair between Tom and Elizabeth played upon the screen. Every touch, every gesture placed so perfectly to create this growing love that echoed within her chest. She rode the wave of their love, so thoroughly enraptured that when the final scene came the ice cream had been set aside, and she hugged the pillow to her chest.

Tom stood on the stage watching Elizabeth walk out of his life for good. He looked down at his hands and flexed his fingers as if realizing she was slipping through them.

"I can't lose you." Tom called out to her.

"It doesn't matter," Elizabeth responded, her hand on the doorknob. "If you can't accept me for who I am, there is nothing left of us."

Tom jumped down from the stage. He opened his arms wide. "I'd give up my entire world for one more moment in your arms. One more night by your side. I want it all. All of you. I want you to have it all. All my love, all my heart, all of me."

Elizabeth turned with tears filling her eyes. His stride ate up the distance between them and he drew her into his arms. Their mouths met and the camera held until the end credits rolled.

That man playing Tom wasn't Chase. Those smiles and looks she'd thought were so similar to the movie weren't. They were smiles Chase only gave to her. The kisses, the touches, the looks, they'd all been real. He hadn't been on-stage. He'd been with her. And when he'd told her he loved her and wanted her to stay, she'd thrown it in his face.

Her hand on her lips, Natalie whispered, "What have I done?" She shrugged out of the blanket and raced to her room.

Chapter Eighteen

A half hour later, Natalie's car stopped in front of the intercom outside Chase's gate. Her heart still thundered in her chest from her mad dash through her apartment, jerking on clothes over her jammies and tying her hair back.

Her hands shook as she coached herself. *You can do this.* She glanced down the street at the man sitting in a car with a camera around his neck. If this didn't work, she would be shooting herself in the foot.

The headlines would read Accountant

Couldn't Take a Hint. But what was the point of being in love, if you didn't at least try?

She pushed the button and squeezed her eyes shut. An eternity passed while she waited, her heart in her hands. Maybe he wasn't in. Or worse, what if he already had someone there?

Fearing the worst, she put the car into Reverse.

"Hello?" The muffled sound of birds came across the intercom with Chase's voice.

"Chase?" Oh, crap, why hadn't she practiced what she was going to say? Everything she'd thought of on the drive over slipped out of her mind and left her fumbling for the words. Mercifully the gate opened, and she didn't have to make a fool of herself to the box on a stick.

The photographer shifted up in his seat and put the camera to his eye. She couldn't tell if he was taking a photo or not. She didn't care. The car pulled through the gates.

A garage door was open, and she drove the

car into it. The garage door closed behind her with finality. She couldn't go back on her decision now, but she didn't get out of the car. Her pulse beat so loudly that she couldn't find the train of her thoughts.

What if he wouldn't forgive her? What if he didn't want her anymore? What if he'd never loved her? What if he laughed in her face? Her eyes burned as tears worked their way to the surface. No, he'd loved her, even if he didn't now. He'd loved her.

The thought gave her strength. She stepped from the car, expecting to find Chase in the garage. She glanced around and didn't see him. She ran clammy hands over the back of her jeans.

Maybe he was in the kitchen. She forced her feet to propel her forward. The kitchen was empty, except for the memories. They clung to her as she moved forward. She could picture him making her an omelet.

She peered into the dining room and spun

through the media room, where they'd spent an evening watching movies and laughing as he'd shared stories from the set. Her curiosity built as she made her way toward the greenhouse. Why not meet her out in the garage? Why force her to find him in his favorite room?

She pushed through the doors and swallowed the thick, fragrant air. The whispered rustling of wings and the discord of birdsongs filled the room. The hot moisture clung to her, and she discarded her sweatshirt, leaving it behind on the path. It didn't matter, nothing mattered, but Chase.

Yanking out the tie in her hair, she let it slip from her fingers to the stone below. The atmosphere of the room pulled at her. The fact that after everything he wanted her in here had to count for something. His favorite room.

She rounded the bend and stared up at the colorful birds perched on branches as if waiting for her. As one they lifted off, flooding her view with rich colors.

Leaving the birds behind, she moved down the path to the gazebo. She could see his shadow in there. Her heart pounded in her chest, and her stomach clenched. She reached up to straighten her glasses only to realize she wasn't wearing them.

She stopped at the door to the gazebo. He stood inside leaning against a pillar. His face was in shadow. Her hand went out to the door frame to steady herself. What if he hated her?

"Why are you here?"

She couldn't take her eyes off his. This was it. She either wimped out or tried for the gold. She cleared her throat. "I'm scared."

"Of what?"

"Of you. Of me. Of the cameras. Of what I feel."

He straightened from the pillar. "Why are you scared of me?"

"Because I can't tell when you are acting." She held up her hand to stop him from speaking.

"My past experiences with guys haven't been great. You know I was homeschooled before I went to college?"

He nodded but didn't interrupt.

"Well, my first boyfriend, Bill, seemed to care about me until after we had sex. The door didn't even hit him on the way out. The guys who pretended to like me to get close to Rachel were even worse. I trusted them, and they lied to me." She still couldn't see his face to read it. "Your performances are award-winning. Theirs weren't."

His body relaxed back against the pillar.

"I never felt for any of them what I feel when I'm with you. I want it to be real." She stepped into the gazebo, dropping her hands to her side. "What I feel is real. I love the way I feel when I'm with you. I love that you take care of me. I love you." Her heart pounded in her chest.

He didn't move toward her.

"How do I know you aren't acting? How can I know what we have is real?"

"You can't know, but you need to trust me. We can't go further with this, if you don't trust me," he said.

"I want to trust you. I want to be with you. I didn't mean what I said that day. I didn't mean any of it." The words could barely make it past the lump in her throat. What if…

"I did." His voice was steady as he stepped forward. Within touching distance, he stopped. His eyes searched hers. She could only hope he would find what he was looking for within them.

"I…" She cleared her throat. Tears sprang to her eyes. "Chase? I love…I love you. Please forgive me."

He didn't move. She stood there open, vulnerable, more naked than she'd ever been in all her life.

"My life hasn't changed." He held back still.

A tear slipped down her cheek. "I know."

His hand lifted as if to brush the tear away,

but stopped. "They'll take your picture and follow you around, waiting for something spectacular to happen."

She caught his raised hand between hers and brought it to her lips. "If I'm with you, it will be spectacular." She pressed his hand against her cheek and closed her eyes, enjoying the spiral of warmth that radiated through her body at his touch.

"Natalie?"

She opened her eyes. He still stood there stiffly. Releasing his hand, she reached up and pulled his face down to hers. Her lips pressed against his, and for a moment he didn't move. Had she been mistaken?

His arms curled around her and dragged her into his body as his mouth claimed hers. A wave of pleasure swept over her, drowning her in sensations of his hard length pressed against her.

The pain of the past week disappeared as her heart filled her chest. She pushed forward to back them into the gazebo. He pulled her back with him until he sat on the bench.

Standing between his legs, she stared down in wonder at the love in his eyes. This amazing man loved her. The feelings inside her were so overwhelming, so pure.

"I love you, Chase." She brushed the hair away from his face and kissed his forehead. "I love you so much."

He captured her face with his hands and brought his lips to hers, but he didn't kiss her. Her eyes opened and stared into green as pure and deep as the leaves of the forest surrounding them. "I love you."

A spear of heat hit her core. He brushed his lips over hers, a gentle back and forth motion. So slowly it was driving her insane. She straddled his lap, placing her knees on the cushioned bench beside his hips. His erection pressed against the juncture of her thighs.

The rich smell of him assaulted her nose, filling her with need, but he kept up his relentless brushing never deepening the kiss and not allowing her to. She rubbed her breasts against the hardness of his chest.

Her brain suffered meltdown as the heat between them intensified, but he did no more than brush his mouth over hers. A low rumble started in the back of her throat as the pressure continued to build within. Her clothes were too tight, and there were way too many layers between their bodies.

She stepped back from the bench. His eyes were glazed as he watched her, but he didn't pull her back to him. Kicking off her sandals, she jerked off her pajama top and shimmied out of her jeans and underwear.

His eyes took in her body, but she was beyond being embarrassed. Her body was on fire, and she needed him. She stalked toward him. She yanked his shirt out of his pants and up. He held his arms up for her to get the shirt off, but didn't help or say anything.

When her breast brushed against his cheek,

his mouth closed over her hardened nipple. She froze as the pulling reached down to her center. Her core pulsed in time with his gentle suction. She caught her bottom lip between her teeth to keep from exploding.

She ripped the shirt the rest of the way off and flung it to the side. Her naked flesh slid against his, warm and moist. He smiled up at her with passion-laden eyes, but he made no move to take over. She wrapped her arms around his chest and pulled him up to stand with her.

Her body pressed into his as she popped open his jean button. Her knuckles brushed against his stomach causing shivers of anticipation to course through her.

She lowered his jeans and his boxer briefs and pushed him back on the bench. She knelt at his feet and pulled the jeans and underwear off the rest of the way.

Crawling her way back up onto his lap, she straddled his hips again. This time nothing blocked her flesh from his and she groaned deep in her throat as the velvet softness of his erection pressed against her stomach.

It'd been too long. A week of longing to be with him. A week of feeling horrible for the things she'd said to him.

Her mouth lowered and captured his. His hands remained at his sides. She would go insane if he didn't touch her soon. Her body was fevered and pulsated with desire.

She slid along him. Her tongue parted his lips and sought his. Her core pulsed with its emptiness as he parried with his tongue.

He leaned over and grabbed a condom from his discarded pants. She guided him to her throbbing center.

Gripping his shoulders, she lowered herself fully on him. Her lips parted and a sigh of relief passed out of them. His mouth captured hers and his hands found her hips.

He didn't move her, just held her. She slid up excruciatingly slowly enjoying the friction of his flesh on hers before lowering herself again. She repeated the process and Chase groaned.

His mouth moved with the desperation she felt and his hands took over her rhythm, sending her soaring higher until all that existed was the pulsating within her. His flesh against hers. His mouth on hers.

Her body clenched around him and her mouth opened in a silent scream. His fingers convulsed on her hips as their bodies continued to strain together. Her fingernails dug into his shoulders as her body rocked into another orgasm.

She could feel his answering pulse within her. He held her body still as he found his own release. Wrapped around him, she opened her eyes and looked down into his.

"I love you." Her voice trembled and was weak, but very, very satisfied.

He brushed her hair away from her face and kissed her softly. "I have never loved anyone the way I do you."

* * *

Chase still couldn't believe Natalie was here, asleep in his bed. He trailed a lazy finger down her back, from her shoulder to her waist where the sheet rested.

He'd been in misery the entire time he was in Ontario, but he couldn't have stayed here. Being close to her was torture. Knowing she was only a car drive away had almost crushed him since she'd made it clear she wasn't willing to be in the spotlight.

She didn't know what she was getting into. She hadn't begun to be pursued by the paparazzi. As an ex-lover she'd been interesting, but to be his girlfriend meant a whole new level of scrutiny. Her nose crinkled in her sleep. He gently brushed her hair off her face.

Would they be able to see what he saw when he was with her? Beautiful, intelligent eyes. A smile that made his heart swell every time she gave him one. When she looked at him, he knew he could do anything, be anyone.

When he'd been gone, he'd lost the peace that seemed to settle over him when she was near. What had changed? Did he really want to question why she was here? Wasn't it enough that she was? That was it, wasn't it? How long could she handle the pressure? How long before she left him for good? How long would love be enough to hold her to him? Would he ever be sure she was here to stay?

He couldn't know, but he didn't want to go back to the way things were before. He didn't want the superficial Hollywood romances. He wanted Natalie.

His fingers tangled in her shoulder-length hair. He leaned down and kissed the pale skin of her shoulder. When he lifted his head, he caught the slight smile on her lips before it disappeared again.

His hand trailed down her spine while he kept careful watch on her face. The little minx was pretending to sleep. His hand didn't stop at the sheet, but continued under and over the curve of her buttocks.

When his hand slipped between her thighs and cupped her, a moan escaped her lips. Gently he stroked her as his other hand wrapped under her to lift her rear up. She rocked against his hand.

The flush of arousal coated her but she kept her eyes closed. Would anyone know the secret beauty who shared his bed? This wonderful creature who dominated his thoughts. Her lips parted.

He grabbed a condom off the nightstand and shifted on the bed until he was behind her raised hips. He replaced his hand with his erection and pulled her up against his body.

"Good morning, sleepy," he whispered huskily in her ear.

Her arm draped up over his shoulder to clutch his neck as he rocked gently against her. "Morning."

His arm crossed her chest, holding her to

him as his other hand found the moist center of her. His fingers slid over her as he continued to rock inside her.

She shattered all around him. Her body shook as she came hard. Her sex clamped down on him. He lost control as his body shuddered in hers.

He lowered them to the bed still inside her, cradling her against his body.

"Definitely a good morning." Her voice was soft as she stretched against him. She gently turned into him to face him. Her eyes reflected his satisfaction.

"Let's go out to breakfast." If this was going to work in the real world, she had to get used to going and being seen. That part of his life wouldn't change.

She stiffened slightly. What if she wasn't ready? Would she ever be ready?

Her body stretched against his again. Her wide, gorgeous eyes smiled up at him. "Where did you have in mind?"

Chapter Nineteen

How could Natalie say no when all the joy had been wiped from his face? Even though she'd wanted to run to the bedroom door and lock it and throw away the key, she knew that at some point they'd have to go out in public. Obviously Chase thought the sooner the better, though Natalie would have preferred to save it for a rainy day.

They sat on the patio of the Polo Lounge at the Beverly Hills Hotel. It was as if Chase was testing her. Thankfully she'd been able to shower and had the sense of mind to run home and change, but she still felt underdressed in jeans, sandals and a light top.

Everyone else was in jeans and T-shirts, but her labels paled in comparison to theirs. Chase sat across from her soaking in the sun. His smile was almost blinding this morning.

She'd managed to hold back the jaw-dropping at some of the famous people she saw sitting around her. They didn't seem to pay attention to anyone around them and completely ignored the photographers across the street.

While Chase would have a nice tanned look to him in any photos that were taken, she would look like she'd spent days in the sun. Her cheeks burned with the feeling of being watched.

Chase leaned across the table and placed his hand over hers. She jerked.

"Relax, Natalie. It's breakfast. No one's going to run up and kidnap you or anything." Chase was obviously joking.

She let out a nervous laugh, but then she glanced around the streets. "Does that happen?"

His hand brushed her cheek, and her focus centered on him and the warmth that engulfed her when he was near. "Just relax and eat. We're just two people having breakfast."

"Yeah, but normally when I have breakfast it doesn't appear in the *Enquirer*. Normally no one notices me at all."

"I notice you." His smile made her insides churn in a good way. "Now eat something, and I'll take you for a walk to some shops."

She gulped as she looked down at the giant croissant on her plate. While Chase had tried to get her to eat a big breakfast, she'd insisted on bread. Bread was less likely to come back up, in her experience.

She picked off small pieces and ate. Chase smiled and shook his head at her before tucking into his quiche. A motion caused her to look up. A group of giggling twentysomethings was heading toward their table.

"Oh, my God, are you Chase Booker?" a petite blonde from the front of the group squealed.

"Can I get your autograph?" A brown-haired girl shoved a pad and pen toward Chase.

He took it and smiled at them. "Who do I make it out to?" He glanced at Natalie briefly.

Was this another test? One of the girls in the back nudged another girl with her elbow and whispered something behind her hand while looking at Natalie. The other girl giggled.

They obviously didn't think she belonged with him. Their laughter and whispered words cut through Natalie. Would it always be like this with Chase? Ignored or ridiculed? Being ignored was fine, but ridiculed behind her back… Her stomach dropped.

Natalie quickly changed her focus back to Chase. He loved her. She loved him. Wasn't that what mattered most? He'd written the autograph and handed back the pad.

"Can I get your picture?" The blonde held up a camera.

"Sure, but then I really must get back to breakfast before it gets cold." He flashed her a smile Natalie had seen a million times in the newspaper.

The girls giggled a thank-you and wandered away. Chase turned back to her. "What's got you smiling?"

Her smile broadened. "Your smile. They think that smile is brilliant, but they've never seen the smile you give me."

His hand reached across to take hers. A flash went off in her peripheral vision, but she ignored it. If she wanted Chase, that had to be part of her life, too.

When they finished up breakfast, Chase took her hand and led her down Rodeo Drive.

Natalie stared in the windows, but when

Chase tried to lead her into Gucci, her feet ground to a halt. His surprised eyes met hers.

"Don't you want to go in?"

"Yeah, but I can't afford anything in there, and I'd feel like Julia Roberts in *Pretty Woman*. Girls like me don't go in shops like that. We stand outside the windows like street urchins and stare at the pretty things." Her gaze shifted to the gorgeous dress in the window. Something she had absolutely no need for.

"What if I wanted to buy something for you?" His hands were on her upper arms, and she longed to be in the privacy of his house or her apartment. Though she relished his touch, she fought the urge to back up and duck her head.

"You don't need to buy me anything."

"What if I wanted you to go to the Oscars with me? Would you let me buy you something then?" His eyes swept over her body like a physical caress.

When he looked at her like that, she'd give

him anything he asked. The street and store disappeared, and it was just the two of them. Her mind cleared. Had he just asked what she thought he'd asked? "What?"

"I asked if you'd like to accompany me to the Oscars. There's no one else I'd rather take with me." His fingers brushed the hair from her face and tucked it behind her ear. "Say yes."

His smile would convince a nun to give up her vows for him. Natalie wasn't strong enough to resist.

"I couldn't afford a dress." She tried to drop her gaze, but his held hers, enraptured.

"I'll take care of it. I know just the person to ask to help."

"When Chase told me he was sending me a project, I'd hoped it would be more than this." The woman pursed her lips as she gestured toward Natalie. "I need a smoke."

Natalie smiled weakly.

The woman sashayed out of the room, leaving Natalie sitting in her office. Natalie pulled out her phone and quickly texted Rachel. *Pls reply. Need dress for Oscars. Crazy Lady went out for smoke. N*

She hit the send button and waited. Her phone beeped in her hand. *So jealous. Insist Vera Wang or Oscar de la Renta.* She dropped her phone back in her purse.

She wouldn't mind switching places with Rachel right now or even to have Rachel with her. The woman, Charity Christian, was anything but charitable. Her dark hair was yanked back so tight it pulled the edges of her eyes out farther than seemed possible. Charity had taken four smoke breaks in the past half hour. Every time the woman looked over at Natalie, she insisted on a cigarette.

Natalie wasn't Alexis Brandt—beautiful, but the ice cream hadn't yet taken its toll on her figure. She didn't have anything to push up, but what she had was all hers.

Charity drifted back in on a gust of cigarette smoke. "I've called around, and I think we might be able to find something. Your eyes are quite nice."

Natalie's lips remained tightly pressed together as she tried not to breathe in the smoke cloud that hovered in the room.

"I know Vera could probably do something or maybe Donna Karan. Stand up again." Charity had picked up a long, pointed stick like people used in presentations.

Unable to disobey the fierce-tongued woman, Natalie stood. Charity's critical eye roamed over every inch of Natalie's body.

"Definitely not red. Especially if you continue to blush like a schoolgirl." Her stick poked at Natalie's lower back. "You have a nice waistline, and you need to remember to smile."

"Umm, is this going to take much longer? I'm supposed to go back to work." Natalie's gaze tried to follow the woman as Charity critically assessed all her faults.

Chase had been thoroughly enamored with her body for the past two nights. Charity's disapproval had nothing on Chase's rich eyes undressing her as she walked across the room. She was doing this for Chase. Somehow she'd manage to put aside her feelings of inadequacy for a while. The dress, the cameras, the Oscars. How on earth does a girl like her get invited to the Oscars?

She kept expecting to wake up or else find herself walking down the red carpet with nothing on. She'd always been thankful to wake up from naked-in-public dreams. But this wasn't a dream; she'd be wearing a dress, shoes and jewelry that would equal her entire year's wages, probably closer to ten years' wages. And she'd be with Chase. A little twitter raced through her.

She definitely had a Cinderella vibe going, except her fairy godmother, Charity, could definitely use some work, along with a breath mint.

Charity muttered under her breath as she whipped out a measuring tape from her pocket and tightened it around Natalie's chest, waist and then hips. She returned to the opposite side of her drafting desk and waved her hand dismissively. "You may go. I'll call you tomorrow and let you know when your fitting will be."

Natalie retrieved her purse. "Thank you." She slipped out of the room and drew in a deep breath of fresh air. She could be everything Chase wanted her to be. Elegant, unabashed, fearless. The butterflies in her stomach kicked up into full flurry. Even if she'd prefer to watch quietly at home, she'd do this for Chase.

Natalie pulled her Honda into Pandora Productions' parking lot and almost pulled right back out. A group of men with cameras lounged across the street, but when her car stopped, they perked up.

The mirror on the visor left a lot to be desired, but her hair hadn't completely escaped her ponytail, and her subtle makeup was not all gone. Her emotions were so jumbled this morning.

She couldn't wait to see Chase, but she didn't want to face the cameras or the other employees who by now knew she'd been at Chase's all weekend. Chase had offered to go with her this morning to the stylist and then drive her into work, but she couldn't let him take her everywhere forever. At some point, she'd have to stand on her own.

A knock on her window threw her heart into palpitations. Her hand blocked her heart's escape through her rib cage. As she turned her pulse increased pleasantly. Chase smiled at her and her mouth curved into a responding smile. He loved her.

She unlocked her door, and he opened it for her.

"Good morning, Natalie." Chase held out his hand to help her from the car.

Her face burned as she recalled exactly how good her morning had already been, and the night before and yesterday afternoon. She slipped her hand in his and a sense of completeness surged through her.

He drew her out of the car, but didn't back up, leaving only an inch between them. Natalie's gaze shot to the cameras that were currently going off. Life would be so much simpler if the cameras weren't at every corner ready to go. She stepped back from him.

"It's okay." Chase's smile was reassuring. "We'll go straight in and not talk to anyone." His fingers linked with hers, and together they walked across the parking lot. "How was Charity's this morning?"

Words flew through Natalie's mind: awful, discouraging, ego wrecking. "Fine. She's going to call me about a fitting tomorrow. When is the luncheon today?"

Chase stopped right outside the door. "Anytime you say 'fine,' it doesn't really mean fine. You mean something bothered you, but you don't want to discuss it."

When she looked at the ground, his finger lifted her chin, and she reluctantly met his eyes.

"It's okay." The words were beginning to sound like he was trying to steady a skittish horse.

"You are beautiful." He brushed a strand of hair behind her ear. "Charity can be really harsh, but she does a damn fine job dressing people. I have no doubts she'll find you the perfect dress, and that you'll look absolutely stunning in it."

His head dipped down to hers, and she quickly turned her head to the side so that his lips brushed her cheek.

"We should really go inside," she said. Her pulse thundered through her veins, and she resisted the urge to turn and taste his minty breath, to forget about the cameras and lose herself in his warmth and taste.

His deep voice in her ear sent little shivers of desire coursing down to pool between her legs. "I'll let that one go. This time."

She avoided his eyes as he lifted his head and opened the door for her. Slipping into the relative safety of the office, she hurried past the receptionist, whose eyes were about to pop out of her head. She managed to make it to her desk without melting into a puddle on the floor. Chase was hot on her heels. Her breath caught at the hot look he gave her.

"I'll see you tonight." Both a promise and a threat lingered in his eyes.

She sank down into her chair as he continued down the hallway. How was she going to concentrate with such a tantalizing offer hanging over her head?

One of the statuesque beauties from the administrative department strutted by and gave her a belittling look. Natalie quickly buried her face into a stack of work.

The hours quickly passed as she concentrated

on work and not on the jealous or curious looks of the amazingly large number of people who had to pass her desk during the day. Chase sent her a smoldering glance as he left for his luncheon with Robert.

"So, trying to get ahead by dating the boss?" The catty voice caused Natalie to stiffen in her chair and tear her gaze away from her computer screen.

The woman could have been a runway model, from her choice in clothing to her makeup to her outrageous look-at-me hairstyle. Her three-inch heels had her towering over Natalie's desk as she looked down her nose.

"I'm sorry." Natalie couldn't have heard the woman properly. This woman had never spoken to Natalie before. She probably thought Natalie was beneath her.

The smile that twisted the woman's face was anything but friendly. "We all try to get ahead by any means possible. But no one has been able to capture Chase Booker's attention. He only dates actresses, not…" She didn't continue but let her gaze slide over Natalie.

If only Natalie were more like Rachel, she'd have a snappy comeback ready and be able to put this wannabe in her place. Instead she wished the warmth would lessen in her cheeks. At least her mouth wasn't opening and closing like a guppy's.

"So how'd you capture the elusive man? Did you get naked in front of him? Did you go down—"

"Excuse me. I'm trying to work here." She glanced down the hall to make sure no one else was hearing this woman. What was this woman's problem?

"Why bother? You have Chase—isn't that what every woman wants?" The woman's eyes shot daggers through Natalie before she pivoted gracefully and strutted away.

Natalie stared after her for a few moments before she stood stiffly and walked down to the bathroom. Is that what everyone thought of her? That she was just trying to get ahead by going to the boss's bed?

She shut herself in the stall and tried to calm her rushing nerves. At least here she was out of sight of all those people. She suddenly felt like the outsider again. A frumpy, short woman among the jungle of beautiful people. Before she'd been beneath their notice, but now she was with Chase. She hadn't considered the reactions from her coworkers when she'd driven to Chase's house. How was she going to cope with this?

The bathroom door opened, and women's voices wafted through the opening. She quickly stood on the toilet without really thinking about it. *What am I doing?*

Just as she was about to step down, the door clicked closed, and the voices became distinct.

"Can you believe the nerve of her?" the woman who'd stopped at her desk said. "I mean, to strut in here with Chase Booker on her heels like some sort of lapdog."

"I know, right?"

Natalie didn't recognize the second woman's voice.

"I heard he's using her to get back at Alexis Brandt for breaking up with him." The first woman's voice got close to the stall door and stopped.

Natalie held her breath and kept completely still. Her gaze was riveted to the doorknob. She'd locked it, but would it hold?

She heard the rustle of fabric, and the woman's heels clicked back toward the sink.

"I think he's doing it as a publicity stunt. Something to slap Hollywood in the face."

Was that all she was to Chase? He loved her. But had it all been make-believe?

"Totally. He can use her, and Hollywood will keep trying to figure out why. That's probably the real reason. Besides she'll sink back into oblivion when he's done with her."

Natalie's heartbeat echoed so loud she wondered why the women didn't hear it.

Her heart tightened painfully as the door closed behind them. Was he trying to prove something to someone by toting her around everywhere? By dressing her up and taking her to the Oscars? Was that some kind of slap in the face of the Hollywood engine?

She stepped down off the toilet. She had to get out of here. She needed to go home. She needed to get away from these people. She waited another few minutes in the bathroom before venturing out into the hallway.

Rushing to her desk, she grabbed her purse and switched off the computer screen. Hoping to avoid the women from the bathroom and everyone else who obviously thought she wasn't worthy of Chase's attentions, she hurried out the front door without meeting anyone's eyes.

Once in the safety of her car, she glanced around. Her eyes stopped on the men with their cameras. How did actors do it? How could they prevent the cameras from catching them when their hearts were on their sleeves and tears were in their eyes?

Chapter Twenty

The luncheon took up more time than Chase remembered. Between the photos and everyone stopping to ask about his latest project or film and, in turn, telling him about their latest project or film, Chase couldn't wait to be near Natalie and not have to worry about the rest of the world.

After saying good-bye to Robert, he dialed Natalie's cell phone on his way to his car, but the call went to voice mail. He called her office number but got voice mail there, too. Tipping the valet, he slipped into his car before dialing the office.

"Pandora Productions," the receptionist said.

"This is Chase. Is Natalie still there?"

"Um, no." There was hesitation in the woman's voice. "She left a few minutes ago."

At the slightly guilty tone of the receptionist, Chase's heart dropped. What had happened while he was gone? Natalie never left work early unless someone told her to. Had he pushed too hard? Was she going to leave him like Becca did?

He hung up the phone without saying another word. He'd have to wait until he saw her to make any conclusions. She seemed so sure that she was ready to be a part of his public life, but he couldn't help wondering when it would become too much. When would she leave him again? He wasn't ready to let her walk out of his life, but what choice would he have?

Maybe this was a mistake. He never should

have started something with someone who wasn't part of the industry. It seemed only a matter of time before Natalie left him for good. He couldn't offer her the life she wanted. Quiet. Unassuming. But he also couldn't stand the thought of losing her again.

Would she go to his place or would she go to her apartment?

He decided to head back to his place. He'd asked her to meet him after work and, if she still wanted him, she would be there. If she wasn't there, he'd have to deal with that when it happened.

He'd given her the gate code as well as an extra garage-door opener. All he could do was hope that she had used them.

Remote controls were evil. Chase had sworn to her that the remote he had for his media center was user-friendly. Apparently not if that user was Natalie. She'd found the DVD for *If*

Only and, after another fifteen minutes, figured out where to put it in.

She had the remote in her lap and stared at the blank touch screen. It was one of those high-end ones that controlled everything from lighting levels to the popcorn machine.

Well, probably not the popcorn machine. She'd just be happy if she could figure out how to turn on the damn remote. She'd tried touching the screen, and nothing had happened. She'd turned it over and all around to see if there was a switch somewhere. She found a few places to plug in cords.

She sighed. All she wanted to do was lose herself in her movie and be here when Chase came home. In his house, she was surrounded by a wall that kept out the outside world. She could pretend that this calm space in his life was all there was. That the cameras, catty women and unwanted attention didn't exist in this house.

Her emotions were completely wrung out,

and the damn frustrating remote wasn't helping to hold back the tears burning behind her eyes.

Whatever the reason Chase wanted her didn't matter. It didn't matter that those women thought she didn't deserve him. He wanted her. He'd made it clear so many times that she was the one he wanted. He'd proved it to her with his words, with his lips, with his hands.… She shook off the desire that spread from the center of her at her unruly thoughts.

Remote. Chase had shown it to her. He'd picked it up and pointed it at the TV, and it had worked. For him. But for her, it obviously wanted a blood sacrifice or something.

She set it down on the chair next to her. There had to be a way to make it all work without the remote. The large screen stared back at her, but no buttons were in sight. The shelves of black boxes with a dozen lights and buttons looked like something from a sci-fi movie. Overall it was intimidating.

"Evil remote." She glared down at it.

"I don't find it at all evil."

She swiveled around to meet Chase's smiling eyes. Her heart filled, her pulse kicked up a notch and the worries from the day seemed to fall away in his eyes.

"In fact I find it a lot easier than dealing with the twelve that came with the components."

"It probably is, once it's turned on."

Chase sat down next to her and leaned across her to grab the remote. His cologne touched her nose. His arm brushed against her breasts, and a shimmer of awareness rushed through her.

"Now, let's see here." He glanced up at her and then down at the remote. Taking his thumb, he placed it in the center of the screen. The main menu came up instantly.

"But I did that." She reached out, and he handed it to her. She squinted down at the menu and touched Play DVD. Glancing up at the TV, she saw nothing happen.

"Here," Chase said and held out his hand. She

held out the remote but he grabbed her hand instead. "Your fingers are probably too cold."

He brought her fingers in front of her mouth and blew hot air across them. "We just need to warm them up." With both of his hands, he massaged her hand.

Her ability to breathe was lost as he made slow circles on her palm with his thumbs. His gaze remained on her hand as he brought each fingertip to his lips and kissed the pad. He cupped her hand and blew against it.

"Now try it." He lifted his gaze to hers.

Her brain had ceased to function, except to send shivers of desire throughout her body. Gently he took her finger and pressed it against Play DVD. The screen came to life.

"There. See, all better." He drew her back against his side and set the remote down. His arms gathered her close, and she relaxed into him. Whatever his reasons for wanting her here, she was here in his arms. He said to trust him, and she did. And even if he was faking it, he was a very convincing actor, because she truly felt loved and cherished and desired.

She settled into him and rested her head against his chest. The steady, rhythmic rise and fall of his chest, and the movie lulled her. His fingers skittered up and down her bare arm.

With the familiar movie in the background, Natalie relaxed. This is what she wanted. Just him and her. No outside world trying to get in.

"Why did you leave work early?"

"It wasn't that early."

He shifted beside her until he tipped her face up to meet his gaze. "You don't normally leave early."

"I…" What could she say to Chase? *I was confused, frightened? I don't know if I can be your girlfriend.*

"You can talk to me." Chase drew his thumb across her lips.

"It was just something someone said." She dropped her gaze to his chin.

"Do I need to fire someone?"

She jerked her gaze up to his at the serious-
ness of his voice. "No. No one needs to be
fired. They just…I just…I don't understand."

"What don't you understand?" He gently
brushed her hair behind her ear.

Her heart hammered against her chest and
her lungs squeezed. "Why me? Out of everyone, everywhere. Why me?"

His gaze softened, and his hands cupped her
cheeks. "Why not you, Natalie?"

She closed her eyes. "Because I'm nothing
fantastic. I'm not fabulous. I'm just convenient."

His lips brushed gently against hers, and
he drew her into his arms. Her head rested
against his beating heart. "You're right. There
are hundreds of women out there that want
me. Who wouldn't think a thing about dating
a man with a hundred cameras in their face on
a daily basis.

"Women who wouldn't mind me being out of

the country for weeks at a time and spending my time with beautiful women."

"This isn't making me feel better," Natalie mumbled next to his chest. His hand stroked up and down her back while his spicy scent filled her nose.

"I've never met someone who makes me feel the way you do. You're beautiful and kind. You make me feel like I could walk on water for you if you wanted me to." He set her back from him and tipped her chin up with his finger.

She couldn't help the tears that swam in front of her vision, making him hard to see. She'd never thought she'd be able to find anyone like Chase, and his words were overwhelming.

"I love it when you smile at me. When you blush because of something I said. When you lean over your desk, poring over numbers as if nothing else exists in the universe. When I wake up and your face is the first thing I see."

His thumb brushed over the tear that spilled

down her cheek. "No one has ever made me feel the way I feel for you. I love you, Natalie."

The music from the forgotten movie crescendoed in the background as his lips met hers. Her heart filled her chest and she wrapped her arms around his neck. Maybe fairy tales did come true.

Rachel arrived home in time to accompany Natalie to Charity Christian's studio to try on Oscar dresses. Chase had offered to go with her, but she wanted him to be surprised. And she wasn't ready to face Charity by herself.

"Do you think she'll have anything in my size?" Rachel said wistfully as she picked up a pair of gorgeous sandals encrusted with sparkling gems.

"Those are worth ten thousand dollars a shoe," Charity's disapproving voice preceded her through the door. Her smoke cloud followed in her wake.

Rachel made an *oh* face and set them care-fully back down with covetous eyes.

"Now, I was able to get a few designers to send some things on such late notice." Every word out of Charity's mouth always made Natalie feel like a naughty little girl.

A small woman pushed in a rack of dresses before shuffling back out. Natalie wished she could get away from Charity as well, but the urge to see the dresses was greater than her fear. She stood and wandered over to the dresses.

Rachel stood beside her and thumbed through the materials. The colors were all fantastic, light creams, blacks, rich shades of gold and brown, deep blues and dark green. Natalie ran her hands over the silk of the dark green gown. Any woman would look stunning in these gowns.

She hadn't dressed up for Chase before. Her heart swelled thinking of him. There had been no prom for her. No best friend going shopping to find the perfect dress. No tux and limo. Now she'd be able to dress in designer gowns and ridiculously expensive shoes and jewelry. And be beautiful, if only for Chase.

"Get undressed, so we can start before I need another cigarette." Charity's voice penetrated the daydream Natalie had been having about Chase in a tux spinning her in circles around a dance floor.

"Right. Where's the changing room?" Natalie looked around but there wasn't a curtain in the room.

"You're in it. Now let's get on with it. You don't have anything either of us hasn't seen before." Charity puckered her lips and gave Natalie a once-over before turning to the rack. "We'll start with this one."

"I think she should try the Oscar de la Renta," Rachel offered. They bantered back and forth while Natalie tried to tone down the blood flowing through her ears. She was barely comfortable being naked in front of Chase, but she wasn't certain she could stand in a room in only her bra and underwear in front of Rachel and the dragon lady.

He may love her flaws, but she didn't need to see the looks from Rachel and Charity. Those looks that questioned why Chase had picked her over any number of women.

For Chase. That's why she was doing all this, for Chase. He was worth every minute of torture because he always matched those minutes with hours of passion that far outweighed the torture. That, and she'd get to wear a gorgeous dress and maybe for once feel like she belonged on the arm of the Sexiest Man Alive.

While the women were distracted with the dresses, she quietly disrobed down to her plain cotton underwear and bra. She'd made sure to wear undergarments that wouldn't leave a line, but she wasn't about to take Rachel's suggestion to go with a thong.

Charity turned and what might have been a smile crossed her lips. "I swear, those clothes should be burned. They do nothing for your figure."

Natalie's face burned. She guessed that was the best compliment she'd ever get from Charity.

"Lift up your arms."

Natalie unwrapped her arms from her waist and held them up while Rachel and Charity lowered a cream dress over her head. The fabric slid against her flesh like a second skin. It was absolutely stunning, but the back dipped down so low, she couldn't help imagining walking down the red carpet with plumber crack.

"This isn't it." Charity stood back with a critical eye.

"Definitely not." Rachel moved to Natalie's side and helped tug the dress off.

They went through the dresses one by one. There were problems with each one. Natalie wasn't comfortable with the cut of some. Rachel wouldn't let her wear anything with a big bow or flower. She swore it was a huge risk.

The fashion police loved it or hated it. Charity just wasn't happy, but Natalie wasn't sure the woman was ever happy.

As they worked their way through the rack, Natalie became less aware of the fact that she was standing half-naked most of the time. Even the dresses that didn't work made her feel beautiful, special.

The green silk dress flowed over her head and settled softly on her shoulders. Thin straps held up the empire waist gown. An intricate lace-and-diamond ribbon wrapped around below her breasts. The layered skirt draped from the ribbon and fell softly to the ground. A fairy princess never looked this good.

Rachel stood behind her looking into the mirror. "Vera Wang certainly knows how to drape a woman."

"It definitely has potential." Charity's critical eye followed the lines of the dress and pinched a few places. "With the right hair and makeup, this could work. I'll pin for the adjustments, and then you'll come back next week to make sure everything fits. We'll also have the hair-stylist here so we can try out everything before the big day."

Rachel smiled a big grin at Natalie in the mirror. "It looks like Cinderella gets to go to the ball."

Chapter Twenty-One

"No, Chase, it's fine. Pick me up from Charity's studio." Holding the cell phone to her ear, Natalie bent her head to the side as the makeup artist worked on her eyes. "I'll see you when you get here."

She snapped the cell phone shut and watched the transformation in the mirror. Braids of her brown hair had been gathered into a diamond clip at the back of her head. The makeup artist performed a miracle involving tweezers and dark eyeliner. It wasn't overdone, but it was more than Natalie had every worn. A mask to hide behind on the red carpet.

Charity paced in the background. Her hand curved as if holding an imaginary cigarette. She puffed out each breath. The woman looked as nervous as Natalie felt.

"You remember how to walk?"

"Yes." Natalie had practiced for the past two days walking and posing in the high-heeled shoes Charity had picked. Her feet and ankles were wrapped in diamonds. Diamonds dripped from her earlobes and a larger diamond fell gently to lie between her breasts over the silk dress. Armed guards seemed like a good idea. Her body's net worth at the moment far surpassed her retirement goals.

"And the pose? You remember that? Never put both your hands on your hips at the same time. Don't face directly into the camera. Don't forget to cock your hip." Charity's words shot out of her mouth, not allowing Natalie time to speak.

"Finished," the makeup artist said, and stepped back as Charity shoved her way in front of the chair. Her critical eyes swept over Natalie's face.

"None of that," Charity snapped.

Natalie attempted to control the blush that had tried to surface. Her hands trembled as she reached up to adjust the necklace after the paper was removed from her neck.

"Beautiful." Charity's face crumpled into that kind of smile. "Stand up so we can make sure there aren't wrinkles on the back."

Natalie straightened, and for a moment was disoriented as she gained a few inches from her heels. Her heart fluttered in time with the butterflies in her stomach.

Charity circled around the back of her and picked at the fabric. She hurried over to a pile of purses and scarves and came back with a small beaded handbag. The lipstick she dropped in it filled the bag.

"This is all you need."

Natalie nodded and stared at the transformation in the mirror. Someone else stared back at her. The dress made her appear taller and was the richest fabric she'd ever touched. Tall and elegant just wasn't her, but if it made Chase happy…

She sighed. Who was she kidding? These past weeks had been the most trying of her life and the most wonderful. Seeing her picture in the magazines Rachel read was disconcerting. Next to Chase, she looked like a small, insignificant girl. But she was with him.

Being in his spotlight was the only way to be in his life. She wasn't sure how much more of the spotlight she could handle. The woman staring back at her in the mirror looked like she could take on this world, but inside Natalie couldn't help wondering if this was who she was. If maybe life would be better without the constant scrutiny.

When one magazine had done a spread of Chase's past lovers, she couldn't help noticing that she was shorter, less blond, less leggy and less everything compared to them. Chase loved her and showed her every night. Her body tightened. But would she be enough? When would he tire of his dalliance with an accountant from the Midwest?

"Chase should be here to pick me up in a few minutes." Natalie felt the need to reassure Charity and maybe even herself that this was real.

"You'll do fine if you remember everything I told you. Just remember the way you present yourself reflects on Chase and on me." Her eyes softened slightly before hardening again. It passed so quickly Natalie wasn't sure it had actually happened. "I need a smoke."

Charity breezed out of the room. Natalie almost sat down but then thought of her dress. How was she supposed to not sit all evening? Would she have to stand in the limo Chase was bringing?

Every move had been rehearsed. Chase had

gone over how the red carpet would be. How he would do interviews down the line while she stood back with a handler or was shown to her seat. One misstep would be played for a decade on *E!* in some red-carpet oops show. She wasn't afraid of a wardrobe malfunction in this dress, but she could easily fall off these heels.

A movement in the mirror caught her eye. Her breath stuck in her throat as Chase stepped into the room. He was positively stunning in his tux. From the devilish glint in his eye to his slightly tousled blond hair, Chase looked every inch a movie star.

His appreciative gaze drifted slowly over her, taking in everything from her hair to her painted toes peeking out from under her hem. Her body flushed where his eyes touched.

He stood utterly still as his gaze returned to hers. "I've never seen anything more beautiful."

She fought the urge to duck her head and

stare at the floor. Chase strode across the room and took her hand. "I'd kiss you but I don't want to smudge your lipstick." He brought her hand to his lips, and little shivers rippled through her.

"You don't look half-bad yourself." Her heart spilled out, making her face pull into a wide grin.

"Shall we?" He led her out the door and past Charity inhaling a cigarette. The limo driver held open the door, and Chase helped her into the back.

After they settled and were on their way to the Kodak Theatre, Natalie's nerves started to fizzle. She was about to walk down the red carpet with Chase in front of thousands of people with cameras everywhere. Live TV. Her chest tightened, and she struggled to draw in a deep breath. Her hands felt soggy as Chase wove his fingers through hers.

"Are you nervous?" His voice startled her in the darkness of the limo.

"Aren't you?" She managed to control the shaking that was starting in her hands.

"I used to be, but I never really had stage fright. One of my teachers told me that old adage, think of the audience naked."

"Oh, God, now I'm going to see everyone naked. I think I'm going to be sick." Natalie struggled with the controls on the door, frantic to get some air.

Chase leaned across and gently moved her hand to the right button and helped her depress it. She gulped in the cool air that floated in. His hand rubbed her back.

"It will be okay, Natalie. I won't let you out of my sight. We'll get through this together." His tone was reassuring and helped to calm her down a little. "Besides, it's not like you'll be the first one to vomit on the red carpet."

Natalie turned to glare at him.

He held his hands up. "It was a joke, love. Only a joke. You'll do fine."

The limo drew to a halt, and Natalie saw

the lights through the tinted window. It was now or never. How the heck had she gotten here? Cameras were prepared to take pictures of Chase and, because she was with him, Natalie.

"I love you." His whispered words and the gentle caress of his lips on her ear sent shivers down her spine.

She turned on the seat to face him and rested her forehead against his. "I love you." She couldn't imagine a day without him in her life. This was just another test, another trial by fire that proved she loved him.

This was his life and if she wanted to be part of his life, she had to be part of this, too. She tried to absorb his confidence. He wouldn't have brought her if he didn't think she could handle it, right?

Her heart slammed against the cage of her ribs as the door opened, and lights flashed in her eyes. A thousand voices rushed into the limo. Her ears ached from the volume, and her hands tried to move toward her ears, but Chase's hold on her hand reminded her where she was.

He brushed his lips across her knuckles and preceded her out the door. Standing for a moment, as cameras created a strobe-light effect in the interior of the car, he turned and offered her a hand.

She stared at it. Could she just sit back and ignore his hand? She wouldn't have to go in front of everyone and make herself available to their ridicule. The butterflies in her stomach threatened to make an escape attempt as she continued to stare at his hand.

Chase leaned in the door. His smile was the one she'd grown to love, the one meant only for her. "Come on, Natalie. What's the worst that could happen?"

She could probably name a hundred things that could happen, each one worse than the next. The one that came to mind was stepping on her hem with her pointed shoes and falling while tearing off the dress. Not only would she be facedown on the red carpet, but also only in her underwear. The heat rose to her face as she met his eyes. "I could trip?"

He clasped both of her hands and tugged gently. "If you fall, I promise to catch you."

She allowed him to help her to her feet outside of the limo. She tried her hardest to ignore the flashing and focused on his smiling face. He was worth it. She tamped down the butterflies as he wrapped one of her hands in the crook of his elbow and gently led her away from the safety of the limo.

The red carpet loomed before her. It glowed bright from the many lights. Colorful gowns swished and dark suits blended to create a beautiful picture. Crowds of people milled along the outskirts and pressed in on the flimsy barriers holding them back. The color left Natalie's face as they passed people she'd only seen on a movie screen. Her fingers clenched into Chase's flesh. What was she doing here?

"Smile, Natalie." His warm breath tickled her ear. "Relax, it's going to be all right."

She forced a smile as they passed a crowd of people chanting the actors' names as they passed. Chase stopped and signed a couple of autographs before moving to the line for reporters.

His hand covered hers on his sleeve, and she looked up. "It will be over soon."

She tried to smile at him, but a fake grin was frozen on her face as the butterflies threatened to burst through her stomach like a scene from a horror movie. His smile softened, and his hand brushed a stray hair from her cheek. His touch energized her. The look in his eyes brought the butterflies under control.

She relaxed her sore cheeks. His hand still over hers, he led her forward again. She barely noticed when Chase nodded at a man who Natalie could only assume was one of the handlers she'd been told about. The one who would rescue her from the reporters and take her to her seat.

When the man returned the nod and turned away, Natalie's butterflies revolted again. She tried to get Chase's attention, but he was pulling her forward to the microphones and cameras. Her instinct to grind her heels was overridden by the paralyzing fear that coursed through her. Besides, if she tried to run, she probably would end up in her underwear as part of the carpet.

She could see Chase's mouth move as he talked to the reporter, but the warning bells ringing in her head blocked out his voice. He'd said she could go with the handlers. He'd said she didn't have to talk to the reporters. He'd said a lot of things. Did his promises mean nothing to him?

Her heart ached as he looked down at her expectantly. What did he really expect from her? She'd never desired this kind of attention. She wanted to be with Chase. He made her feel things she'd never felt before, but this mass panic in her body was not one of the things she loved.

A flicker of concern went through his eyes, and he turned and told the reporter who designed her dress and mentioned Charity. An eternity went by as she stared helplessly at the red light on the camera. Chase gently tugged her arm to lead her to another line.

She knew the pictures tomorrow would show her with a panicked look on her face. Chase would be humiliated. She already was humiliated. Why had she agreed to this? This wasn't her. If he really wanted her for who she was, couldn't he see that?

Instead of getting in the line for the next reporter, Chase led her to a relatively quiet area out of the spotlight. Her shoes sparkled in the lights. Something she didn't think she'd ever be able to do.

He blocked out the red carpet with his broad shoulders and drew her into his arms. The

fuzzy, warm feelings of love chased the spec-
ters of fear back into their corner. She leaned
into him, drawing from his strength.

Why couldn't it just be the two of them? Why
did the whole country have to be involved in
their love affair? He pushed her back slightly.
He wanted her to look up, but she was afraid.
She couldn't keep up this act. She wasn't built
for this kind of situation. She had no delusions
of what she looked like. She was ordinary,
which was fine for everyday life, but someone
like Chase needed one of those women, the
ones who were extraordinary.

"Natalie?"

Unable to resist his soft, deep voice, she
shifted her gaze up.

"I have to do the interviews. I want you to
stay with me. Do you want to stay with me,
or do you want to go to your chair?"

She nibbled on her lip. Was this a test? Would
she fail if she went to her chair? Would he be

disappointed if she went to her seat? Could she stand to go back to the cameras?

"This is a part of who I am." Chase's eyes were intense as they gazed down into hers. "It's not going to go away. I don't want to do it alone. I want to share this with you. I want to share all of me with you."

She drew in a deep breath. "I want to be with you, Chase. I just…" She dropped her gaze back to the floor.

He lifted her chin with a finger and dropped a brief kiss against her lips. "Then share this with me, Natalie. Come and be a part of it. Don't hide in the corner. Trust me. I won't let you down. I promise."

Her eyes glittered with unshed tears. No one had ever loved her like Chase did. She wasn't willing to let that go without giving it a chance. She forced herself to nod. Her reward was a glowing smile from Chase.

His lips brushed over hers. His gaze traced her lips, checking to see if he'd smudged her makeup before he led her back to the line. She'd finally realized what the worst thing that could happen was.

She could lose Chase.

Chase felt like it was the first time he'd taken the stage. His heart hammered in his chest. Adrenaline rushed through his veins. Natalie stood stiffly beside him, but the look of panic was gone.

He'd seen it in her eyes, known she was weighing her options. Knew he was pushing her, but if he didn't now, what would happen when he was on set and someone showed her a picture of him with his costar? He didn't want to go to his movies and the award shows alone. He wanted to experience it with Natalie.

He automatically answered the reporter's questions, gave his dazzling smile and continued on, all the time aware of his little accountant at his side. Her smile wasn't quite as bad as it had been, but it was definitely forced.

Maybe if he'd reminded her of how much he loved her. Maybe if he'd told her that whatever happened he'd still love her. Maybe if he'd told her how beautiful she was. Maybe she would have relaxed enough.

This was something she could get used to. When they got home tonight, they could share some ice cream and watch the award show and laugh at how nervous she'd been over nothing.

"And what about you, Natalie? How are you enjoying the evening?" The woman reporter put the microphone close to Natalie's lips.

Chase held his breath and squeezed her hand with his. It was like he was the one on the spot, not her.

"It's all very lovely." Natalie's voice was slightly higher pitched than normal, but at least she'd managed to talk. Her cheeks had a slight flush to them. Chase smiled down at her as she answered the "who are you wearing" question.

Her hand released a little from gouging into his arm, and he led her to the next interview. He leaned down and whispered in her ear, "That was great, love."

She flushed, but didn't look up at him as they confronted the next reporter.

"And now I'm here with Chase Booker and his girlfriend, Natalie Collins," Rick Jones said to the camera. He turned and stuck out his microphone. "Chase, your movie *Night Blooming* has been nominated for seven awards. How do you feel about your chances tonight?"

"I think all the nominees are wonderful across the board. We're up against some tight competition. It should be an interesting night." Chase kept Natalie tight against him.

Rick asked Natalie who she was wearing, and Chase watched Natalie relax slightly and answer. As she spoke, he couldn't help but realize how lucky he was to find her.

He led her away, noticing how her body shook next to his. He'd pushed her enough for the evening. The interviews were over for now. They stopped for a picture before heading into the theater.

The usher escorted them to their seats. Chase took Natalie's hand in his and brought it to his lips.

"You did wonderfully, Natalie."

She blushed softly and smiled. "It wasn't as awful as I thought it would be."

"No falling or puking. I think that's a pass."

Her gaze roamed the crowd. Her expressions captivated him as she recognized actors she'd seen in movies or TV. Chase had already med most of them, either through his parents or during his own career.

"Chase," Robert said as he and Alexis sat beside them. "Natalie, you look stunning tonight." Alexis had chosen a daring gown. Obviously she was aiming for a best-dressed nod. Even worst dressed would help get her the attention she craved.

"Good evening, Chase." Alexis pouted her full lips his way. "I'm so glad you decided not to bring me. Robert is such a fine escort." She ran her hand over Robert's arm.

Robert gave Chase a helpless look. Robert typically avoided bringing anyone to shows. He was a confirmed bachelor and rarely dated. Women tried all the time to get him, but he remained cool and aloof.

Natalie's face tilted his way. Chase knew he was hopelessly lost when it came to Natalie. He'd been trying to break her all week. Clubs, dinner and finally the Oscars. Maybe he was wrong to push her, but he wanted all or nothing. He'd rather lose her now than years down the road when it would be harder to let go.

He followed her gaze to see Shannen Matthews, his costar from *If Only*, standing beside his chair. Chase rose from his seat.

"Chase, how are you?" Shannen leaned forward and kissed the air beside his cheeks.

"Good, good, and you?"

"Missing London. I swear L.A. gets hotter every year." Shannen's blond hair brushed his sleeve as she turned her head and waved at someone.

"It has been a warm year. Natalie is a huge fan of *If Only*." Chase glanced over his shoulder at Natalie, but she wasn't looking at him.

She nodded in Natalie's direction. "I must find Bill. We'll catch up at the after party." She kissed the air again and sauntered farther down the aisle.

Chase sat down as the lights began to dim. Natalie's hands were clasped on her lap. He reached over and plucked one of them. He folded his fingers in with hers and listened to the opening act.

"Have you worked with Shannen Matthews after *If Only*?" The tentative whisper tickled his ear.

"Yeah, we're supposed to do something in the future. Some sort of period romance," he whispered without taking his eyes off the stage, where they were announcing Actor in a Supporting Role nominees.

"Oh."

He glanced over at her, but her eyes remained riveted on the stage. What had that been all about?

The ceremony continued. Natalie clapped and watched along with the rest of the crowd, but something was off. Something in the way she smiled alerted him that something was wrong. Her fingers restlessly pinched at her satin dress. Her cheeks were stained pink and her lips were drawn tight. Had he done the right thing by bringing her? Was it too soon?

Becca had been a teenager when she left him. Natalie was a grown woman. Her shyness was one of the things he'd fallen in love with. Her reluctance to be brought into the spotlight charmed him. She made him happy, and she was trying so hard.

She'd taken everything he'd thrown at her this week. He'd stopped worrying that today would be the day she'd leave him. He'd begun to hope that they could make this last. That he could make a life with Natalie even though she wasn't an actress.

Maybe he could make it up to her by skipping the after parties and just going home. They could cuddle up with some chocolate ice cream, and he could show her once more how much he loved her.

Chapter Twenty-Two

Natalie laced her fingers together. Chase loved her. Would that be enough? They hadn't talked long term, but she couldn't begin to imagine a life without him in it. But to have to brave this scrutiny every year…every month…every day….

Her normal, boring life would change. Not that it hadn't already. After all, she sat next to Chase Booker at the Oscars. Never in a million years would she have imagined being here. She would have never considered it a possibility or wanted it.

The goals she'd set for herself had nothing to do with fame. A good career, a solid man, a few children, retirement. Nowhere in her future had she wished for cameras intruding on all the moments in her life. Strangers wouldn't have wanted to know what she was doing. But as long as she was with Chase, her life would be open season for reporters and so would her children's lives.

Her eyes drifted to Alexis's beautiful profile. Chase had dated Alexis. The woman personified sex, from her lush curves to her to-die-for lips. When Chase went to his next movie set, a woman as gorgeous as Alexis would be waiting for him.

They'd kiss passionately because Chase always got the woman in the movies. How would Natalie's kisses measure up? How would he feel coming back to L.A.? To her? Natalie

Collins, petite brown-haired wallflower. How would they ever have a private life? Chase's life was public. Had always been public, would always be public.

His smile was radiant as he watched the next presenter. He did look like Prince Charming. Unfortunately, she didn't qualify as Cinderella.

He reclaimed her hand. Her traitorous body tingled in reaction to his touch. His eyes met hers. How long before he realized he'd made a mistake? How long before he wound up in someone else's bed because she wasn't cut out for this kind of life?

"Are you all right?" Chase ran his fingertip down the side of her face, leaving a trail of bittersweet desire behind.

She tried to steady her wayward thoughts. All relationships were built on trust, and she trusted Chase. Even though she preferred a quiet life, she loved him.

"Natalie?"

The crescendoing music kept time with her pulse as an Oscar winner left the stage.

She smiled at Chase and touched his cheek. "I'm fine."

His eyes narrowed, but the next presenters began their speech for Best Picture. Chase and Robert's faces appeared up on the big screen as *Night Blooming* was announced.

"And the Oscar goes to Chase Booker and Robert Addler for *Night Blooming*." Applause sounded all around them.

Chase's face cleared of all the concern in a heartbeat as he flashed his winning smile at the camera. He leaned close to her. "We'll talk when I get back."

He moved to the aisle and strode toward the stage with Robert. The music had stopped, and Chase and Robert were getting ready to deliver their speech.

"We'd like to thank the Academy." Chase's voice filled the auditorium. "There are so many people who were part of this film and helped to make it happen."

He continued congratulating the whole cast and everyone involved in production, and she'd never felt more proud in her life. Her heart filled with love and warmth for Chase.

At the end of his speech, he turned to face her and gave her that smile that was hers. When he smiled at her like that, she was willing to give up everything, just to be with him. She cheered with the rest of the crowd as he was ushered backstage. Everything would be okay.

Alexis leaned over the empty seat. "They'll be a few minutes backstage. We can head out if you'd like." Her smile was predatory, but Natalie assumed it was always that way.

"Sure, but I'd like to find the restrooms first."

An usher happened to overhear her and escorted her to the bathroom.

The doorman opened the door, and Natalie swept into the relative emptiness of the foyer.

Natalie froze at the landscape beyond the doors of the theater. Though it was night, the exterior of the Kodak burned as bright as if it were noon. The rich and famous posed and paraded outside.

Alexis hadn't waited for her out here either. Breathing deeply, Natalie moved toward the doors. It couldn't be any worse than before. Except then she'd had Chase with her. Being next to Chase made her feel more beautiful, made her feel like she belonged.

She stepped out onto the red carpet and stopped to scan the crowd for Chase. Her gaze flowed over the other actors and zeroed in on Chase.

Her smile froze as she saw Alexis curving into his side as the camera flashed. Suddenly everything clicked into place.

Alexis wanted fame and attention. She didn't need coaxing to get into the spotlight. Someone like Alexis would be there for him and look beautiful doing it. She didn't mind the attention. She didn't want a quiet life. She didn't want simplicity. She'd fit in Chase's life, where Natalie was a square peg trying to shove into a round hole.

Tonight she felt gorgeous with the dress, jewelry, makeup and shoes, but tomorrow she'd go back to being just Natalie. How long would just Natalie be enough?

No, that was stupid. Chase loved her. Natalie trusted him. He'd said he didn't want anyone but her, and she believed him. For now, she was who he wanted to be with, but what about a month from now? Six months? A year?

Alexis turned and pressed her lips to Chase's cheek for the next photo.

Natalie spun as her heart plummeted. This wasn't who she was. She wasn't strong enough to watch her man pretend to be in love with someone else. She wasn't strong enough to walk toward him and claim him from Alexis. But somehow she'd find the strength to walk away.

She jerked open the doors and went back into the theater. There had to be a back exit. She picked up her skirt and hurried across the tile floor.

The door slammed open behind her.

"Natalie?"

Oh, hell, all he had to say was her name, and she wanted to stop and let him convince her she was wrong. That she deserved to be with him. That she could take the pressure of being his girlfriend.

His hand closed over her shoulder. She squeezed her eyes shut at the warmth in his touch and the feelings that swirled around inside her.

"Natalie, are you all right?" Chase didn't spin her around or move in front of her, and for that she was grateful.

She couldn't say what she needed to say if she lost herself in his green eyes. Opening her eyes, she stared at the red exit sign that would lead her back home.

"Who are we kidding, Chase?" Natalie's eyes filled with unshed tears. She kept her voice steady. "You don't need me. You need someone like Alexis. We don't make sense."

"I don't want Alexis. I want you." He slowly turned her until she faced him.

She kept her eyes on his tie knot. "For how long?" she whispered.

His fingers tensed on her shoulder. The pain was slight compared to the hurt curled up in her chest.

"Natalie..."

What was going on in his head? Was he going to thank her for calling it quits because he hadn't wanted to hurt her? An unchecked tear slipped down her cheek. She drew in a deep breath and waited for his reply.

"This is who I am. It won't go away. The Alexises will always be there. The cameras will always be there. The speculation will always be there." His fingers fell from her shoulder, leaving her cold. "I thought you trusted me."

Another tear escaped down her cheek. She had moments before the floodgates opened. "I can—" Her eyes connected with the paparazzi outside the window. A small crowd had gathered. Nothing was private, nothing was sacred. Life with Chase was life in a fishbowl. If she walked away now, her life would go back to what it had been before, quiet, unassuming, boring, safe.

He could go back to his fabulous women who wouldn't feel like hurling on the red carpet. Who wouldn't need so much reassurance to get through one evening.

His finger caught one of her tears.

She took another deep breath and stepped back. Her heart shuddered. "I wish I could, but I can't, Chase." Her voice trembled and the words barely left her lips. "I just can't." The tears welled unbearably. Before he could say anything, she spun on her heels and raced toward the beckoning exit sign.

She almost wished she'd fall, but when she

reached the door, she turned for one last look. He stood where she'd left him. She couldn't let him hurt her. She had to be the one to leave. The door slid shut behind her.

Chase let her go. What else could he do? He couldn't force her to stay. He couldn't change who he was, who he had become. The box in his pocket weighed heavily on his mind.

He'd wanted to share forever with her, but it looked like their fifteen minutes were up.

A hand clapped over his shoulder. "Tough break." Robert moved to stand beside him. "We've got pictures to take."

Chase watched the door she'd vanished behind. Every second it stayed closed, the hollowness in his chest grew. He'd known better. He'd known it would end this way.

Knowing didn't ease the tightness. "I'm going to take that role."

Robert nodded. "The last-minute replacement."

It had sat on his desk for the past two days as he debated whether their relationship was strong enough for him to leave for a few months. Apparently, it hadn't been strong enough.

"Yeah, I'll fly out Monday morning." Chase turned back toward the theater doors. He'd do what he did best, lose himself in a part.

"Do what you need to do, my friend."

"What are you going to do?" Rachel tucked her feet up on the couch.

"I can't quit my job. I haven't even been there two months. We can't afford not to have my paycheck." Natalie swept through the room with a pile of pillows and sheets. She'd remade the bed, but his scent still stubbornly clung to a few things. A trip through the washer should solve that problem.

It was well past midnight, but she didn't think she'd ever be able to sleep again. Rachel had waited up for her when she used the phone in the limo to call and blubbered in Rachel's ear. The tears were gone now. Just an emptiness remained, and no amount of crying or ice cream was going to fill that hole.

"He probably won't be at work tomorrow. All the after parties last well into the morning." Rachel clicked on *E!* and hit mute.

Natalie headed for the DVD player and hit the eject key. "You're right. It's not like he's around that much. I'm sure he'll start work on something soon, and I don't have to work late anymore since the new CFO starts Monday. I'll just sit at my desk and do my work."

She lifted *If Only* out of the player and pushed it back into its case. She'd walked away from Chase Booker, and even though her heart was broken, she felt like she could do anything. She opened the freezer.

Rachel glanced over her shoulder. "Are you sure you want to do that?"

"Yes, I'm sure." Natalie put the DVD case with Chase's face in the freezer and took out a carton of chocolate ice cream. Even though she'd gone back to her boring life, not everything could stay the same. She dropped the ice cream in the trash and rubbed her hands on the back of her sweats. "I'll get by."

"You'll do fine. Even if you see him, I'm sure everything will be okay."

For a week, Natalie's heart jumped every time someone walked past her desk. No one really talked to her, which was par for the course. Robert had called her into his office to make sure she wasn't quitting and restated that they both thought she was good to have on their team and would hate to lose her.

She'd reassured him that she wasn't going anywhere. After all, where could she go? She had two months of experience, right out of college. She sighed and tabbed back over to the spreadsheet. Chase was in London for the next month or so, which should give her plenty of time to get over their short affair.

Why did it feel like more than just a month had passed? Why did her bed feel empty? And her heart ached for what? A month? She shook her head. There was no room for such thoughts anymore. She'd get over Chase Booker and act as if nothing happened.

Her phone had been turned off to external calls, which had been a blessing. Everyone wanted to know what happened to the flash affair between Chase Booker and his lowly accountant. She brought her lunch and only left with Robert walking her to her car.

An e-mail pinged in the background. Natalie automatically flipped over to the e-mail. It was from Jared Anderson. Her mouse hovered over the delete key, but curiosity got the better of her.

If you need to talk to someone, off the record, give me a call. I've been following Chase for years and have some information that might help.

Might help what? Make him not famous?

Make her not shy? Make her trust in him beyond the tabloids? The dull ache stayed in her chest, constantly reminding her that she'd lost the only man she'd loved. Not because of who he was, but because of *who* he was.

The reporter couldn't tell her anything that would change her mind. This was the life she'd chosen. She hit the delete key.

Chase guided Amanda Rogers into the dining room.

"It really has been a pleasure working on this film with you, Chase." Her finely manicured nails pawed at his suit jacket.

"It's a great movie. I was glad the lead dropped out." He smiled down at her. After years of acting, he would have thought he'd learned to hide his true feelings, but he could feel the cracks on the edge of his smile. Hopefully no one else could tell.

He held out her chair and took the one beside her. The rest of the cast and crew were already seated around the table at the old castle where they were filming. The period piece wasn't exactly helping him get over his relationship with Natalie.

He played a hero trying to save the heroine from the clutches of an evil sorcerer. Every time he stared down into Amanda's beautifully overdrawn face, he saw Natalie's pert nose, wide brown eyes and constant blush.

"Do you think you'll stay in London after the filming ends?" Amanda had been dropping hints all week about starting an affair or a flirtation or anything.

He was confident Natalie was probably hearing that he and his costar were involved in a tawdry love affair. When in reality, he lay in bed at night staring up at the ceiling knowing Natalie was awake and wondering what she was doing. Robert had told him that Natalie had decided to stay on at Pandora Productions.

"I'm not sure what my next move will be." Chase waited for the wine to be poured. "We still have a few months of filming." A few months for him to get over Natalie. Then he could get back to dating women who were used to fame.

"To getting to know each other better." Amanda's red lips curved into an inviting smile. She held up her glass of white wine.

He wished Natalie were here as he tapped his glass against Amanda's. He would have loved to show her England and Europe. They could have escaped up to Scotland for a weekend. Maybe he should take what Amanda was offering. Maybe then he could get Natalie out of his head.

"Chase?"

He lifted his eyes to Amanda's bright blue ones.

"You aren't over her, are you?" Her usually plastic face was soft and knowing. "It's okay, you know. If you want to talk about it?"

Chase glanced around the table. Everyone was

involved in their own conversations, enjoying the wine and the food.

"Look, Chase, we need to stick together here. You can't go all moony-eyed on me every time someone mentions her."

"I don't go all—" He turned to catch Amanda's teasing smile.

"I'm not above stealing a man from another woman, but not when he's desperately in love with her. So why don't you tell me about it?" She stabbed a piece of carrot and chewed on it with her attention completely on him.

"She's not one of us." Chase took a swallow of wine.

"You mean she's an alien or something." Amanda's eyebrow rose.

"No, she's not used to being in the spot-light."

"Oh." Amanda chewed another piece of carrot before responding. "So, she's like me before I became an actress."

"I highly doubt that. You probably loved at-

tention. She'd prefer to stay in the background."
Chase smiled softly, remembering Natalie's
shyness.

"True. I was made for Hollywood. But so
what? Why should she adore the spotlight?
What's wrong with having someone in the
background cheering you on? Instead of having
to manage two careers?"

"Because it's part of my life, it's part of who
I am. If she can't be in the light with me, when
else am I going to see her?" Chase's fork clat-
tered on the plate.

"My God, Chase. What a snob you are." Her
eyes twinkled in the candlelight. "You'd give
up a chance at happiness because she didn't
want to be in front of the silver screen. Do you
know how many actors and actresses would
kill to find a relationship where they knew the
person was after them and not using them to
get a leg up in the business?"

Chase stared down at his plate. Her words
echoed through his head.

She placed a hand on his arm. "Love doesn't come around all that often in this business. If you've got it, why the hell would you let it go?" Her words rang through the hall.

The din of conversation stopped. Chase looked around the table to all the eyes turned on him. Could it really be that simple? Would it all be right if he went back and asked her to be with him any way she wanted? Just as long as she was in his life?

"Well?" Amanda's voice drew his attention back to her. "What are you waiting for?"

"Yeah, Chase. Go get her," came from the end of the table.

Chase pushed back his chair. "I'll see you all in a few days."

Natalie pushed up her glasses as she tried to concentrate on the binder in front of her. Her contact had torn that morning, and she'd had to put on her glasses at work. Things had gone pretty much back to normal.

The tall, model-like employees continued to use the hallway as their personal runway except it didn't bother her like it had before. She just kept working.

When she was working, she could keep her mind off Chase. Wondering who he was with? If he missed her? Rachel had assured her that Chase and Alexis weren't back together, which made her heartache worse.

Even if she wanted to live in his fishbowl world with him, she'd burned that bridge. There would be someone for her, but no one would be like Chase. He definitely had been worth the scrutiny, but it had been too much.

She tried to focus on the papers in front of her. What she wouldn't give to get away? Unfortunately, she hadn't been at Pandora long enough to ask for vacation so she could recapture her focus.

A shiver of awareness went through her. Startled, she looked up, but no one was in the hallway. Her nose tickled with the scent of Chase's cologne. Her heart jumped in her chest, hoping for more than just his scent. She tamped down on her wayward heart.

Someone must be wearing his favorite cologne. Chase was somewhere in England shooting a film with some actress who had likely taken Natalie's place in his bed. Her stomach pinched at the thought. She knew the tabloids weren't always right, but it didn't hurt any less.

She needed one of the other binders from down the hall to figure out this last reconciliation.

She hurried to the file room, still marveling at the way the office cleared out after four on a Friday afternoon. If she could get these last few numbers into her spreadsheet, she could e-mail it to the CFO and leave for the day. Not that she had anywhere important to go.

She shoved her glasses back up her nose and

scanned the sides of the binders. Of course, it was the top shelf. She grabbed a stool and pulled it over. Stepping up, she closed her hand over the binder.

"Do you need a hand?" Chase's voice sent tidal waves of joy pulsing through her body. The heat from his body scorched her back.

Natalie couldn't move. Her arm was still slightly above her head, even with the stool. Her mind blanked, and her heart skipped. "Uh, no. I've got it."

He leaned into her back, and his hand closed over hers on the binder. She closed her eyes against the assault to her senses. The instinct to lean back into him almost overrode her common sense.

Her heart pounded in her ears even as it clutched in her chest.

"Natalie?" His soft words lifted the hair around her ear.

Every nerve in her body strained with the need to turn and fling herself into his arms.

She couldn't, though. She couldn't be what he needed.

"Forgive me." His words reverberated through her being. His hand closed over hers and brought her knuckles over her shoulder to his lips.

A gasp of air escaped her at the sensation of his lips on her flesh. Unable to fight her impulses, she spun. She had to see him. Her eyes drank in the sight of him. With the stool they were face to face. A slight darkness underscored his eyes. His hair was a bit more tousled than usual, but he was just as gorgeous as he'd ever been.

His words sunk in. "Forgive you?"

His hand brought hers back to his lips, and he kissed each of her knuckles. "I never should have pushed so hard. There's only one woman I want to be with, and I don't need to share her with the press."

His hand caressed the side of her face and trailed down to her neck. "You ground me.

Keep me real. I love you. I can't promise life with me will be easy, but I want you to share it, with or without the cameras. Can you trust in my love for you?"

"What are you saying, Chase?" Her aching heart eased and began to fill her chest with hope.

"What I should have said at the Oscars. However you are willing to share my life—even if you want to stay in the background—I want you there. In my life, in my bed, in my future." He pushed up her glasses. "Will you marry me, Natalie?"

A thousand things rushed through her mind. A thousand what-ifs were stomped down by her heart. She couldn't imagine living without Chase. Her heart had ached every day they were apart. He was worth giving up her private life.

Her hands cradled his cheeks. "I trust you, Chase. I want to be a part of your life. I love you." She kissed him.

He drew her into his arms and captured her lips with his. The weight on her heart lifted. Anything was possible with this man by her side.

Epilogue

Natalie stood silently staring at the reflection in the mirror. The dress was simple, but elegant. Her hair was pulled up with ringlets left loose to float around her face. Her makeup was subtle. She'd never felt more gorgeous.

"No, Charity. It's fine." Rachel's gaze met hers in the mirror, and Rachel rolled her eyes. She continued to talk into the phone, "No, it's not wrinkled. Woman, it's called a vacation. I've got everything on this end. Go relax somewhere." Rachel snapped the phone shut.

"Okay, where were we?" Rachel picked up a slip of paper. "I think we got everything on Charity's checklist."

"I'm surprised she sent you a checklist." Natalie turned and smiled at Rachel.

"I'm not." Rachel set the list down. "But you're gorgeous, Natalie. Every man out there is going to wish he was the one standing there."

A short rap on the door sounded before it was cracked open. "It's time."

Rachel grabbed the bouquets and studied Natalie's face intently. "I'm so happy for you."

Rachel pulled Natalie into a brief hug before handing her a bouquet.

For a moment, Natalie's butterflies took flight in her stomach. After this, Chase and she were headed to Hawaii for a week, where they could be alone. The butterflies settled and she followed Rachel out the door.

Her father took her hand as she entered the church, which normally sat a few hundred. The pews were full, and people were standing along the sides.

As they stepped forward after Rachel, Natalie's eyes connected with Chase's. His smile took her breath away, and even though the paparazzi were outside the church waiting, she couldn't be nervous.

Her future waited for her at the end of the aisle. A future that included the man she loved and trusted to keep her heart safe.

When her father passed her hands to Chase's, Chase leaned down next to her ear and whispered, "I'd give up my entire world for one more moment in your arms. One more night by your side. I want it all. All of you. I want you to have it all. All my love, all my heart, all of me."

Her eyes misted over, and she leaned into him. "I want you for who you are. I trust you with my heart. I love you, Chase Booker, whether the spotlight is on or off."

His finger brushed aside the tear on her cheek.

He brought her hand to his lips and pressed a kiss to her knuckles. "Forever."

"Forever." She turned with him to step up the stairs to the awaiting minister. Ready to spend every day in the fishbowl as long as Chase was by her side.

* * * * *